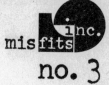

misfits inc.

no. 3

growler's horn

mark delaney

PEACHTREE

ATLANTA

To John Delaney,
my Uncle Jack—
When I was thirteen, you gave me a guitar for Christmas
and helped me find the music in my fingers and in my heart.

A FREESTONE PUBLICATION

Published by
PEACHTREE PUBLISHERS LTD.
494 Armour Circle NE
Atlanta, Georgia 30324

www.peachtree-online.com

Text © 2000 by Mark Delaney
Cover photograph © 2000 by William P. Gottlieb, Library of Congress/Ira & Leonore
S. Gershwin Fund

Book and cover design by Loraine M. Balcsik
Composition by Melanie M. McMahon

Manufactured in the United States of America

10 9 8 7 6 5 4 3 2 1
First Edition

Library of Congress Cataloging-in-Publication Data

Delaney, Mark.
    Growler's horn / Mark Delaney. -- 1st ed.
      p. cm. -- (Misfits, Inc. ; no. 3)
    Summary: The theft of Jake's clarinet leads him and his friends to investigate
other mysterious occurrences, including the theft of millions and the disappearance
of an up-and-coming jazz musician.
      ISBN 1-56145-206-8
      [1. Musicians--Fiction. 2. Mystery and detective stories.] I. Title.
PZ7.D373185 Gr 2000
[Fic]--dc21   99-086977

E-mail the author at: misfitsink@aol.com

table of contents

Acknowledgments

Special thanks to:

Detective Alex Bancroft, Orange County Auto Theft Task Force, undercover officer and brother-in-law extraordinaire,

For illuminating the secrets of handgun maintenance and unveiling the mysteries of bugging devices.

And

Mr. Bryan Henson, Band Instructor, Hickman County High School, Centerville, Tennessee

For giving me—and Jake Armstrong—the knowledge Jake needed to repair an antique clarinet.

If a mistake appears in these pages, don't blame these guys!

Prologue

Karl Logan held the gun as though it were sacred. He ran his finger along the barrel, holding it so that the chrome caught the sunlight and flashed in his eyes. Then he pulled back the slide and began to take the gun apart.

The day was warm. Karl sat on a large redwood deck at the rear of his Caribbean home, a glass of flavored mineral water on the table next to him. The deck faced an expanse of private beach where, only a few steps away, the ocean splashed against an acre of gray rocks and white sand. Karl watched the waves a moment, savoring the way they foamed just before dying out, then went back to work. He laid a lint-free cloth along his tabletop and reached for his bore brush.

The gun was a chrome-plated, 1911 Colt .45 military pistol, and it was quite valuable. Many years ago Karl had purchased it from a collector. Now it was Karl's favorite—and only—weapon. He wore it in a leather shoulder holster on those late nights when he was working. Other than a tool belt, it was the only addition to his

2   work uniform: black pants, black turtleneck, black ski mask.

It was a point of pride for Karl that he had never fired the gun except in practice. To fire it would be to admit that a security guard or a policeman had gotten close enough to him to be dangerous, and Karl would never allow himself such a failure. Indeed, he had made a pact with himself. If Karl ever found himself in a situation that had gone so far out of his control that firing the gun was necessary, he would retire. Until that inevitable moment, the gun's clean glossiness would remain a symbol of Logan's perfection as a thief.

Seagulls squawked in the distance as Karl laid out the pieces of the gun and began cleaning them. He sprayed cleaner and lubricant where needed, and he used a bore brush to reach inside the gun's barrel. He held the empty barrel up toward the sun so he could see how clean it was. Even a grain or two of sand might alter the flight of a bullet.

When he was satisfied that he had cleaned the gun thoroughly, Karl reassembled the pieces and placed the weapon back in its holster, then laid the holster carefully on the table.

A chirping sound came from Karl's cellular phone. Any bright sixth grader with a working knowledge of electronics could listen in to an analog cell phone conversation, so Karl's phone was a state-of-the-art digital model, to which Karl had added a built-in encryption program. In his line of work, he had to have secure communications. He reached for the phone and, with a quick motion of his wrist, flipped down the mouthpiece. "Yeah?"

"Um—hello? Is this—?" The voice on the phone hesitated, fumbling for words, then suddenly began speaking as if reading from a script. Most potential clients sensed they had to speak carefully, or they would never find Logan again. "I...I got your name from Mr. Sarducci. I have a job for you."

Karl leaned back in his chair and rested his bare feet on the tabletop. "I'm listening."

"Next Sunday, there will be a private auction held in Bugle Point—involving mostly innocuous household items, nothing of obvious interest. However, three of the items have...a history...and they might prove to be embarrassing to me. I want you to obtain them."

Karl grunted. "An *auction?*" He rarely turned down work, but a request to bid at an auction was almost insulting. Perhaps the caller did not understand what Karl did—or what Karl earned for what he did. Logan toyed with the offer a moment.

"So first I'll need you to—"

"I don't like the *smell* of it," Logan interrupted. "Why all the cloak-and-dagger stuff over an auction? Why not just bid on the items yourself?"

"That's none of your business."

Okay, Logan thought, so the caller didn't want to play out the whole story. Well, it wasn't the first time a potential client had a secret or two, but Logan had long ago

4 learned that such secrets could only lead to problems for him. "Not good enough," he said.

And if the story doesn't get better in about thirty seconds, he added silently, *I'm hanging up.*

The voice spit out its answer. "I'm trying to *hire* you. I have the money, and my connections allowed me to find you. That alone should prove to you that I'm serious. I want the job done, and that's all you need to know. My motives are my own and are, as I said, *none of your concern.*"

Logan chuckled and pressed the "end" button on his cell phone, canceling the call. He tossed the phone back onto the table.

Twenty seconds later it chirped again. Logan waited, allowing it to ring several times before he picked it up.

"Please don't hang up on me again," the voice whispered, chastened.

"Listen," Logan said. His tone remained quiet and even, sending the message that he and he alone would dictate the terms of any bargain. "To do a job effectively, I need to know everything—including the reason why I'm doing it. If you don't want to tell me what's behind this, fine—but find yourself another thief."

The voice waited a very long time before answering. Logan heard a deep drawing in of breath, then a low, sighing hiss as the breath was released. "All right, then. I can't bid on the items myself," said the voice. "The auction house will take names and addresses from the successful bidders. If I were to bid, or if someone connected to me were to bid, these items might be traced to me." The voice continued, a hint of panic slipping into its tone. "*You* can't bid on them, either. You'll have to get them some other way, and quickly. Please…I will fax you the details later today, and at that time we can negotiate your price."

"Sunday is too soon," Karl said. "To steal the items before the auction, I would have to scout the location, learn what security measures are in place. You've given me no time."

"That's up to you," said the voice. "Do whatever you think is necessary, but get the items."

So, the client wasn't just expecting Karl to bid on the items and deliver them to a pre-arranged place. Now the job began to make sense. Tracking the items through the auction to their new owners and stealing them without leaving a hint of his presence—perhaps this job was indeed worthy of him. Karl began to think he might even find the challenge *entertaining*. In his own mind he decided to accept the contract, but he had one more concern to address. Clients, Karl knew, understood little about the art of theft, about the time and effort Karl required for preparation. A thug would hold a knife to his victim's throat and demand what he wanted, but thugs, almost without fail, wound up in prison.

"Who knows?" the voice went on. "If you're a jazz aficionado, you might even find something you'd like for yourself."

6   Karl bristled. He never stole for himself. During his career as a thief, he had developed a very precise and strict code of behavior. Living by his word, and by the rules he had set for himself, was a point of honor for Karl Logan—honor this client could not begin to understand. Karl received payment for his work, and he bought what he wanted—like this beachfront house— with the money he earned.

But as a professional, Karl would forgive the slight. "Very well," he said. "My basic operational fee is a quarter million. Half up front, half when the job is over. Then we add on to that the price we negotiate on the stolen items themselves. Understood?"

"Understood," said the voice.

Karl nodded and closed the phone. *Jazz aficionado?* he thought. *Bugle Point?* He wondered what he was getting into. It sounded too simple. He cautioned himself that simple jobs had a way of making one careless.

The time factor concerned him. If nothing else, he would have to allow the objects to be auctioned off and only then take the proper time to plan. That would mean three thefts instead of one, unless he got extremely lucky and the same buyer bought all three items.

Karl shook his head. Worrying was a fool's hobby. Everything, especially the worries, could wait until he had the full picture. After the fax arrived on his secure fax line, he would evaluate the information and negotiate his price. Then Karl would make his concerns clear to his client.

He took another sip of mineral water and put away his gun. Later, he decided, he would do some yoga stretches, throw on his running shoes, and have a jog down his private beach.

Friday

eugenia "Byte" Salzmann had been thinking about the stupid flower all morning.

She sat in the lunchroom at Bugle Point High School. The nylon bag containing her laptop computer hung from her shoulder, and her elbow pressed against it, clutching it to her body. Her backpack lay on the seat next to her. Her lunchbag, made of quilted fabric, sat open on the Formica tabletop. Inside the lunchbag was a bottle of fruit juice, a chunk of some kind of twelve-grain bread her mother had bought in a health food store, and a Tupperware container filled with spinach salad—a good, healthy lunch. Byte had no complaints, other than the fact that, as was often the case when she was alone in the crowded lunchroom, her stomach was in knots and she wasn't very hungry.

Mostly she was thinking about her friends.

And that stupid flower.

The flower captivated her—like a song you hear once in the morning and can't keep out of your mind the rest of the day. Earlier this morning, her history class had watched a film on the Vietnam War. One bit of footage showed a college student walking up and down a line of National Guardsmen, all of whom carried rifles and stood at attention. The young man, to Byte's delight, stuck a flower in the barrel of each rifle. A crowd of anti-war protesters stood nearby, and one of them, a girl hardly older than Byte herself, had painted a daisy on her cheek.

The daisy had wrapped itself around Byte's thoughts the remainder of the morning. Somehow all the images she had seen of that period—the young man plugging the rifles with flowers, Neil Armstrong's footprint in the lunar dust, Robert Kennedy smiling and flashing a peace sign, a thousand college students simultaneously holding matches to their draft cards—all of these pictures seemed to swirl and coalesce into the single daisy that girl had painted on her cheek. Byte's eyes followed the daisy until the young woman slipped off the edge of the screen.

Now, as she waited for her friends, she thought again of that daisy, and her hand began digging into the outer pouch of her computer bag. *There it is.* Her fingers closed on a fat, plastic pen with four different colors of ink.

Then she reached into her backpack and fished out a compact mirror, popping it open to reveal the reflection of a girl with straggly, dark-blond hair and wire-framed granny glasses perched on the end of a sharp nose. Byte crinkled her nose, and the glasses crept up a bit, allowing her to see more clearly. Then she took the pen, clicked on the red ink, and watched herself in the mirror

10 as she drew a rose on her left cheek. The young woman in the film liked daisies; Byte liked roses.

She used green ink to fill in the stem and the leaves. Working quietly, she tuned out the rumble of the lunchroom, until a titter of laughter finally interrupted her. Byte looked up from the mirror and saw three girls sitting at a nearby table. The girls stared at her, at the pen hovering in her fingers, and at the bright red rose on her cheek. Then they looked at one another and burst out laughing again.

One of the girls gave an exaggerated nod of appreciation. "Ooohhh, *very* stylish," she said. Another girl whispered, "She's so weird," loud enough that Byte could hear her.

Upon hearing the words, a brief pang of loss struck Byte. She missed her friend Robin Sutter, who had transferred to a science and math magnet school. It would be nice to have Robin here now, to have someone to talk to about the history film and the rows of guns with the flowers in their barrels and the girl with the daisy on her cheek.

Byte clicked the pen again and jammed it back into her bag. Ignoring the girls, she eyed herself in the mirror and nodded, satisfied.

Then, from a distance, she heard a familiar voice over the chattering in the lunchroom. "It's not mind reading," the voice insisted. "It's observation and deduction."

Byte looked up and waved. Peter Braddock, brushing a dark lock of hair from his eyes and grinning from behind a pair of owlish glasses, waved back. He was the leader of their group of friends, who called themselves Misfits, Inc. At the moment he was talking to another Misfit, Mattie Ramiro.

"Umm hmm," Mattie was saying. He was looking up at Peter, but his fingers toyed absently with a playing card. Byte watched as the card vanished from Mattie's fingers, reappeared, then vanished again.

"Yeah, but when you do it, it *seems* like mind reading," Mattie said as they made their way closer. "That's what's so cool about it. It's like magic, see? Show me again. Hi, Byte!"

Peter smiled. "Yeah, hi!"

The two boys sat across from Byte, setting their brown-bagged lunches in front of them. Mattie put his arm on the table, and Byte saw the corner of the playing card poking out from the sleeve of his jacket. She smiled and pretended not to notice.

"Hey, guys," she said.

Peter turned to Mattie, who was still gazing at him hopefully, and sighed. "All right," Peter said, "I'll explain it one more time. You observe and deduce. Look closely at what's around you and figure out what it means. Like this—" Peter looked across the lunchroom, and his eyes settled on the group of students waiting in the food line. "Okay, see the girl in the denim skirt?"

"Yeahhh...." Mattie said.

"I've never seen her before," Peter went on, "but right off the bat I can tell you that she's a freshman, she's recently moved here from Texas, and she's a very bright student."

Mattie stared at the girl, then threw up his hands. "How do you *do* that?"

12   "I *observe*," said Peter. "Look at the stack of books she's carrying. See the paperback on top? *To Kill a Mockingbird*. Required reading for ninth graders. Now look at her science textbook. It's the one they use in the honors-level classes. So I know she's a freshman, and I know she's bright."

Byte found herself suddenly interested in the conversation. "Okay," she said, "we'll give you that, but what about the Texas part?"

Peter pointed to the girl. "Look at the front of her jacket."

Byte looked closely and for the first time noticed the gold pin on the jacket's breast. The girl stood near enough that Byte, once she made the effort, could read the pin clearly. It was a large Texas star surrounded by the words I Love Texas.

Peter grinned. "Texans are known for being proud of their state."

"Okay," said Byte. "I'm suitably impressed."

Peter shrugged, doing a very poor job of hiding his pride.

Just then another girl walked up to the girl in the denim skirt. "Hey, Cassie," she said, her voice ringing out in a clear Texas accent, "thanks for holding my stuff." The girl in the denim skirt cheerily handed the stack of books to her friend, then peeled off the jacket and gave it to her.

Byte and Mattie looked at each other and burst out laughing.

"Hey, knock it off," said Peter, unable to hold back a smile himself. "I never said I was perfect."

Now that her friends had arrived—and were tugging eagerly at the wrappers around their sandwiches—Byte pulled the spinach salad from her lunchbag, popped open the lid, and stabbed her plastic fork into a chunk of tomato. "Okay," she said, "we have to figure out what we're going to do for Jake."

"Jake" was Jake Armstrong, the fourth member of Misfits, Inc. Two weeks ago Jake, as a clarinet player in the Bugle Point High School jazz band, competed in the first of several competitions that, by the end of the school year, would determine which high school band stars would win state-level prizes. Jake had twice before represented B.P.H.S. as a soloist. Today Mr. Janson, the band teacher, would announce the names of the students who would have featured solos at the competition's next level.

"Well, we know he'll make it," Mattie said. The playing card reappeared in his hand, snapping as it popped into view.

Byte sighed. "I hope so," she said. Neither Peter nor Mattie had mentioned the flower on her cheek. She hoped Jake, at least, would notice it.

Just then a pair of hands slipped over Byte's shoulders and clamped down over her eyes. The hands, the size of small baseball gloves, covered more than half her face. She knew it was Jake. Jake was tall, well over six feet, and weighed about two hundred pounds. Even when he stood behind you—even when his hands came down over your eyes—you knew it was Jake.

"Hi there, soloist," she said, tugging the hands away and turning around.

"Hey, Jake," said Mattie, "watch this...." Mattie fumbled with the card again, trying to make it vanish, but it popped from his fingers and hit him in the forehead. "Wait, wait," he said.

Byte grabbed Jake by the arm and pulled him down onto the bench next to her. "Okay," she said, "no holding back. Tell us all about it. What did Mr. Janson say?"

Jake was quiet for a moment.

Byte had envisioned this scene all morning: Jake sauntering up to the lunch table, his mouth drawn up in that shy sort of half-smile he had. He would be holding that little Superball in his fingers, the one he always carried with him, and he would bounce it against the floor, swallowing it in his huge hand when it ricocheted back up. Then he would smile at the Misfits, give a humble shrug, and say, "Made it."

If Byte had not already lived this moment in her mind, she might have noticed sooner that Jake's expression was flat, his eyes vacant. He looked stunned.

"Jake?" she asked.

He did take out his Superball then, but instead of bouncing it triumphantly against the floor, he twirled it in his fingers, as though examining the scuff marks on its surface.

"I didn't make it," he said quietly.

"*What?*" Mattie cried.

Byte felt her stomach churn. In her mind, the honor was *already* Jake's.

"What happened?" asked Peter.

"I got an honorable mention," Jake went on, "but I won't be the featured soloist." He cleared his throat and swallowed before continuing. "Mr. Janson pulled me aside after the announcement. He told me that my instrument limited me, that my playing really deserved better than the clarinet I've been using. We've been talking about it for a month now. The school can't afford to buy me a new clarinet, and my mom and dad sure can't afford one. I have to find a way to buy one myself."

"I don't get it," said Mattie. "What's the problem? I thought your old clarinet sounded just fine."

"Oh, please," said Jake. "It's a *composition* clarinet." He folded his arms like a giant sulking child. Byte stared at him, gathering only that a composition clarinet must somehow be inferior to some other kind.

Jake must have noticed the confusion on her face. "A composition clarinet," he said, "is made of—well, I guess you could almost call it pressed sawdust. Like particleboard. It works fine, and it doesn't sound bad, but its tone will never improve. I could be the best clarinet player in the world, and its tone will always be the same."

Peter nodded. "So you want a—?"

"—I want a *solid wood* clarinet." Jake saw the blank look on Peter's face and drew in a deep breath. "Okay. Wood has a mellower tone. And the tone only improves with age. Right now I'm stuck. I can't get any better until I get a better instrument. Mr. Janson is right. Do you *know* how frustrating it is to pick up my clarinet to

16 play a difficult passage, and know I can do it, but the stupid instrument *can't*? Everything is riding on this—the state band awards, maybe even my chances for a scholarship."

With that, Byte's head snapped up. She had not thought that far ahead. More than anyone she had ever known, Jake Armstrong had framed a plan for his life. Byte knew Jake's goal was to win the state band competition—at least once—to cement his chances of getting a scholarship to Berklee College of Music.

She turned toward him. Jake was staring at the wall. "Well, then," she said, "I guess we'll just have to get you a solid wood clarinet. Will you have a chance to solo in the later competitions?"

Jake shrugged. "Maybe. Probably." Then his head lowered. "I dunno."

"All right, then," said Peter. "So we'll get you one."

"Yeah, no problema," said Mattie.

Jake looked up and let out a short laugh. "Hey, thanks—really—but they're pretty expensive," he said. "I've been nosing around here and there, and I haven't found one I can afford."

Byte stood up then, leaving her lunchbag and backpack on the table, but reaching for the bag containing her computer.

"Going someplace?" Peter asked.

"The library," Byte said. "Be back in ten minutes." She left without a word of explanation.

When she returned exactly ten minutes later she held

a computer printout in her hand. She laid it on the table in front of Jake.

"What's that?" Mattie asked. He reached for the paper, but Jake slapped his hand away and frowned, scanning the sheet.

"The local newspaper is online, and I found this press release," Byte boasted. "Am I good, or what?"

"Doesn't the library subscribe to the paper?" asked Mattie.

Byte poked her tongue out at him. "Don't be snarky. Besides, a real newspaper doesn't let you do a keyword search, so *there*."

Jake scanned the page in front of him.

EVENTS CALENDAR

LOOKING FOR MORE?

Search 1,000,000 of the world's best sites.

Search tips.

Submit your favorite site.

<u>Today</u>   This week   <u>Next week</u>   This month

Estate Sale
On Sunday, at 1:00 p.m., an auction will be held at the estate of Mrs. Helen Morton.

Included in the auction will be an assortment of antique furnishings, Depression glass items, and vintage jazz music equipment.

Mrs. Morton is the widow of Jerome "Growler" Morton, the jazz clarinetist whose meteoric climb was interrupted by his mysterious disappearance in 1957.

For reservations, directions, or other information, contact Starlight Auctioneers, 555-1212

OTHER LINKS

Antiques
Auctions
Depression glass
Estate sales
Jazz
Music
Musical Instruments

< BACK   NEXT >

18   "Well," said Jake, "I don't know."

Byte tapped her finger on the sheet. "It says right here, 'vintage…jazz…music…equipment.'" Her finger hit the sheet four times, punctuating each word. "And the guy was a clarinet player. Can't hurt to call the number and ask if they're selling one."

Jake nodded. "Yeah," he said, warming to the idea, "yeah, okay."

The bell rang a few minutes later, calling students to their afternoon classes. Byte gathered her belongings, ready to drag herself to fifth period biology.

As she and the others headed toward the lunchroom doors, she felt Jake's hand on her shoulder.

"Hey…hey, Byte?"

She turned to face him, stepping aside so other students could pass. "Yeah?"

"Well," said Jake, "I just wanted to say thanks." He waved the paper containing the auction information. "I mean for this."

Byte shrugged. "Hey, Misfits stick together." She pointed at the sheet. "Don't lose that."

Jake's eyes widened. "Right. *Right.*" He quickly folded the sheet and tucked it into his math book, on top of a pile of papers that looked to Byte like chatty notes from other students, sheets full of Jake's aimless doodlings, and his math homework assignment.

"Oh, and Byte?" he said as they began walking again. "Yeah?"

He tapped his finger against his cheek. "Nice flower."

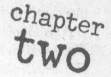
Sunday

While waiting for the auction to begin, Jake Armstrong daydreamed that he was standing in front of the display window of Garlick's Music Store, his eyes locked on a brand-new clarinet. He sighed. The clarinet was the color of polished coal, and its gold-plated keys threw off light like Christmas garland. Jake, because he was controlling this little fantasy, allowed himself to walk into the store and touch the clarinet. He raised it to his lips, positioned his fingers over the keys, and began to play....

Jake felt a tugging at his shirtsleeve.

"Hey," said a voice. "Earth to Jake...."

Jake's daydream crumbled, and he was suddenly aware that Garlick's music store was miles away. Instead of preparing to play a beautiful new clarinet, he was standing on someone's back lawn, and the gold-tinged instrument at his lips was instead a lightly spotted banana he had swiped from a fruit basket. More than a dozen people milled around him, nibbling on miniature sandwiches and pouring pink, foamy punch into crystal glasses. Jake folded his arms and tried not to grumble.

He turned in his chair to see Peter, Byte, and Mattie staring back at him. Right now Mattie, the youngest member of the group, was crossing his arms and frowning, clearly annoyed. Byte and Peter stood nearby, also looking irritated. Jake realized he'd been tuning them out, as he often did when his mind was preoccupied.

"About time I got your attention," said Mattie. "You still bummed out over the clarinet at Garlick's?"

Jake nodded, silent. Yesterday the Misfits had gone to the music store, just to let Jake drool over a fine clarinet. The purpose of the visit was to psych Jake up for the auction, to make him feel as though, in only a day or so, he would be the proud owner of a glorious instrument like this one. But the clarinet's price had been higher— far higher—than Jake could afford, and handling the instrument had only made him more and more certain of impending disappointment.

"Oh, Jake," said Byte, "it'll work out."

Peter nodded. "Besides," he said, "let's look at things logically. How much is the clarinet at Garlick's?"

Jake made a noise in his throat that sounded like a growl. "Thirty-five hundred dollars."

"And how much money do you have?" asked Peter.

Jake glared at him. "Six hundred."

"Okay then," said Mattie, "so there's no *way* you can buy it, right?"

"Right," Jake muttered.

"Then the way I see it," Mattie said, "you should be happy. You might get a clarinet today that's just as good. And this used clarinet might be within your price range."

Jake grumbled.

Byte frowned at him. "Jake," she said, "you could be just a *little* positive. We've done the research; the most you can afford is a used clarinet. There's a *chance* you'll get this one for six hundred, and you might really like it."

Jake remained silent. He wasn't quite ready to admit that today just might turn out to be a good day.

He took the crumpled advertisement from his pocket and gazed at it. He had called the phone number yesterday and learned that, yes, a clarinet would indeed be among the auctioned items. Thrilled, he had made a reservation. His experience at Garlick's, however, left him more depressed than ever. *So what if the auction includes a nice clarinet?* he wondered. *Could I ever afford it?*

"Let's head over to the seats," Byte suggested. "We're late enough already."

Mattie glared at her. "Hey, I said I was sorry." He froze, posing like a male fashion model. "You don't get to look this good by throwing yourself together."

Jake laughed, and the four of them walked across the back lawn of the Morton home, arriving at the spot where the auction house had set up a podium and a public address system. Lawn chairs stood in neat rows, and the Misfits sat, eyeing the roped-off area where potential buyers could view the items for sale. Each item, called a "lot," was numbered. By looking up the lot number in a brochure, buyers could read a detailed description of the item.

Since Jake and his friends had arrived late, they had not had a chance to view the clarinet up close. The rope had gone up five minutes ago, and a woman—"Nancy," according to her name tag—had urged the visitors to seat themselves. Jake had strained at the rope, studying the instrument as best he could from six feet away. Now, as the auction was starting, Jake fumbled through the brochure and reread the description: Clarinet, c. 1897. Teak w/silver trimmings. Fair condition. *Estimated value, $800.00.*

What exactly is fair *condition?* Jake wondered.

Byte interrupted Jake's thoughts. "Looks like they're starting," she said.

A man with sparse black hair and a pencil-thin mustache strode to the podium. He cleared his throat, tapped on the microphone, then spoke in a clipped, British accent. "Ladies and gentlemen," he began, "thank you for your prompt arrival. We shall begin immediately."

Jake looked around at the other guests. Most were well-dressed men and women who looked to be in their fifties or sixties, probably wealthy antique collectors. Another man—a short, stocky guy who nervously slapped his checkbook against his palm—had more businesslike intentions. He had arrived in a dented panel truck marked McCollum's Antiques.

Jake looked at his friends. Mattie was humming quietly to himself, gazing at his hand as he practiced rolling a quarter across the back of his knuckles. Byte smiled at Jake and gave his arm a squeeze. Peter sat hunched in his seat, his eyes flickering back and forth across the small crowd of buyers, no doubt taking quiet measure of each.

Again a horrible feeling of doubt washed over Jake. "All of a sudden," he whispered, "I'm starting to think that my six hundred dollars isn't going to go very far."

"Lot number one...." called the auctioneer.

Hours seemed to pass before the auctioneer came to lot forty-seven, the clarinet. Jake sat forward in his chair, holding his breath for a moment as the auctioneer glanced down at his stack of index card notes. The man peered over the lenses of his glasses.

"Lot number forty-seven," he said, "is a clarinet, circa 1897." He went on to read the rest of the description, and it was time for the bidding to begin.

"Don't start too high," whispered Peter.

"Um," said Jake, raising his hand, "two hundred?"

"Two hundred!" echoed the auctioneer.

Jake jumped in his seat, realizing that he had actually placed a bid and the bid had been accepted.

"Two-fifty," said a voice from behind him.

"Two seventy-five!" another voice said.

Jake threw a panicked glance at his friends, and when

24 the auctioneer suggested a three hundred dollar bid, Jake meekly raised his hand.

"I have three hundred," said the auctioneer.

A long, uncomfortable silence hung in the air, and the auctioneer began tugging at his bow tie.

"Why does he look so nervous?" asked Jake.

Peter leaned in toward Jake to whisper. "The auction house's fee is based on a percentage of the total sales. The less people bid, the less pay this guy gets at the end of the day."

"Got it," said Jake.

"I have three hundred," the man repeated, and he raised an eyebrow when the crowd remained silent. "Oh, come, come, people," he said. "Surely you recognize the value of this fine instrument, once owned by the late Growler Morton himself. Do I hear three hundred and fifty?"

"All right," said a gruff voice, "three-fifty."

Jake spun around to see who had spoken. Two chairs behind him sat the guy who owned the panel truck. McCollum, or whoever he was, grinned at Jake and shrugged his shoulders.

"Three hundred and fifty," said the auctioneer. "Do I hear four hundred?"

When Jake reluctantly raised his hand, the auctioneer looked *much* happier than he had a moment earlier. "I have four hundred," he purred.

"Four-fifty," said the antique dealer.

Jake gritted his teeth. He had not wanted to spend all his money if he could help it, but yesterday's trip to

Garlick's had shown him what a *real* clarinet sounded like. "Five hundred," he called.

He turned around again and saw that the antique dealer was hesitating. McCollum slapped his checkbook into his palm a few more times, then opened it to glance at the balance. He frowned.

"Hmmm… okay. Six hundred," he said.

Jake started to raise his hand and bid again, but then he realized what the antique dealer had said. *Six hundred.* Six hundred dollars was all the money Jake had. He could match the antique dealer's bid, but he could not go higher. He would not be able to buy the clarinet. Jake let his shoulders collapse as he slid down in his chair.

"The bid is six hundred," said the auctioneer. "Going once.…"

Jake looked at his friends and saw the sympathy on their faces. The crowd sat quietly for a moment, waiting to see if Jake would match the antique dealer's bid, but their stares only wrenched his insides into a knot. He knew this auction was his last hope. Where else in the world would he find a six-hundred-dollar antique clarinet?

"Going twice," said the auctioneer.

"We'll keep trying the pawn shops," whispered Mattie.

"Sure," said Byte quickly. She fingered the nylon shoulder bag that contained her laptop computer. "Later I'll try the Net again. We're bound to find something."

"And the newspapers," added Peter. "Each of us will keep an eye out."

Jake said nothing. What *were* his options? He could sell his car, if he could get anything for it. He could hope that his band teacher had connections, or that another band student with a good horn was deciding to give up the clarinet for some reason.

Jake groaned. He was kidding himself. It was hopeless.

The auctioneer raised his wooden gavel, readying himself to bring it down with an echo of finality. "And—"

"Wait!" shouted a voice.

It was Mattie.

Jake, stunned, turned slowly and looked at his friend. "What are you doing?" he hissed.

Mattie slugged him in the shoulder. "Buying some time," he hissed back. "Don't just sit there—think of something!"

Jake raised his head and sat up a little straighter. An idea did come to him. It was silly—it was downright embarrassing, actually—but Mattie was right. Jake had to *try*.

"Guys," whispered Jake, "how much money do you have on you?"

Mattie shrugged, shoving his hand in his pocket and pulling out some coins. "Just the change from when we went out for lunch."

"I have two dollars," said Byte.

"A five," said Peter.

Jake held out his hand. "Give it here," he said. "I'll pay you back later."

They all scrambled to fish through their pockets. In a moment, Jake was holding a fistful of change and several wadded up bills wrapped in a string of pocket lint.

The auctioneer studied the teenagers, twirling his gavel impatiently. "Do we have a bid?" he asked.

"Um, yeah—hang on," said Jake, eyeing the money. "Six hundred and *seven* dollars, and…" he hurriedly counted the change in his palm, "seventy-five…eighty-five…eighty-seven cents." He looked back up at the auctioneer. "That's my bid."

The guests tittered. One man near Jake chuckled more loudly than the rest, but Jake ignored him. Instead, he turned around and met the antique dealer's eyes.

McCollum had heard the bid, of course. He looked at Jake, but he didn't laugh. He sat back in his chair, his finger tapping against his chin, and he regarded Jake with the cold, dispassionate look of a hardened businessman. He remained silent for several seconds, but then the hard look fell away and he offered Jake a smile. He raised his fingers in a mock salute as if to say *it's all yours.*

Jake pumped his fist in the air. "*Yes!*"

The auctioneer, nonplussed, tapped his gavel against the podium. "Very well, then," he said. "Six hundred and seven dollars…*and eighty-seven cents*…going once, going twice, and sold to the four teenagers with the rather loud voices."

A little while later, Jake and his fellow Misfits stood by Jake's car as he set the clarinet case on the hood. He studied it a moment.

"It doesn't look like six hundred dollars," he said, shaking his head.

It was an older style of instrument case, made not of molded plastic but of leather stretched over a wooden frame. The leather was worn, faded in several places, and it peeled up from one of the corners.

Jake took in a deep breath and let it out. "Well," he said, "here goes."

He tugged at the latches, and the case popped open. There, broken down into its four parts and resting in old velvet, was the clarinet. Jake picked it up. It was definitely solid wood—Jake could tell by the weight—but it looked every bit as old as it was. The keys were dull and gray, tarnished to the color of an old cooking pot. Two or three of them were bent so that they didn't cover the holes in the clarinet properly.

Jake, crestfallen, stared at the instrument and wondered if it would play at all.

Mattie bit his lip. "It looks great!" he exclaimed. "Doesn't it? I think you definitely did the right thing. I mean, six hundred dollars for this piece of musical equipment, now that's a deal...."

Jake silently looked over his purchase, but Byte and Peter frowned at Mattie.

"Okay," Mattie admitted, "so maybe the one at Garlick's *is* a little nicer...."

"Mattie!" Byte practically yelled. "Enough already!"

"Fine!" Mattie shot back. "I was only trying to help."

Jake gave him a sad smile. "I know you were," he said. He turned back to the instrument and sighed.

The Misfits returned to Jake's house, tossing off quick hellos to Jake's folks before racing upstairs. Jake, who had remained silent during the drive home from the auction, spread the pieces of the clarinet on a coffee table and began to repair the instrument.

As Jake worked, he heard a sharp *snap*. Mattie had reached for Jake's chromatic tuner, undoubtedly with the aim of taking it apart to see how it worked. Peter had slapped his hand away.

"Oh, it's okay," Jake said. "Thing's not working right anyway. Maybe he can fix it."

Mattie pocketed the tuner for a later inspection. "About time I got some respect around here," he grumbled. He then satisfied himself by pulling a deck of playing cards from his jacket pocket. He fanned them, then practiced a one-handed shuffle. He grinned at Peter. "Wanna see a trick?"

Peter was engrossed in the current issue of *Chess Life* magazine and didn't bother to look up. "You know I always guess how you do it," he murmured.

Mattie riffled the deck. "This time, Ramiro the Magnificent will astonish you," he said.

Byte slipped over to the couch. She sat quietly for a while, then Jake felt her finger tap him on the shoulder. "I didn't want to interrupt," she said, "but how bad is it?"

"Not sure yet. I'll know in a minute," he said.

He studied the disassembled pieces. Strips of cork lined the joints, but the cork was dry and flaking. Jake

30 tore it off with his fingernail, then began the painstaking process of replacing it. He took a strip of cork, trimmed it to the correct length, then glued it down. His fingers pressed into it, smoothing it into a tight ring. To check the fit, he tested it against another piece of the barrel and discovered that the cork was too thick. He gently filed it down, adjusting the thickness until the two pieces fit just tightly enough to prevent air from escaping.

Most high school band students would not have undertaken such a repair, preferring instead to turn their instrument over to a technician. But Jake was not a typical band student. For three years he had worked closely with Mr. Janson, his teacher, staying after school and learning everything he could about the maintenance of band instruments. Jake understood that an antique instrument might need such repair and had borrowed the necessary materials from his teacher.

Mattie tossed down the deck just as Peter was about to select a card. He pointed at Jake's handiwork. "What does the cork do?" he asked.

"It just grips the wood so that the pieces of the clarinet stay together," said Jake. "The grease will help seal it, and it makes it easy to take the clarinet apart and put it back together."

Next Jake studied the bent keys. "The damage to the keys looks worse than it actually is," he announced. "Clarinet keys are made of soft metal, and they bend easily." He braced his thick fingers against the bad keys and, one at a time, carefully bent them back into position. He then took his mom's silver polish to the keys and rubbed away the tarnish. To Jake's happy surprise, the keys were indeed silver. They shone, and Jake had to smile when they caught light from the window and momentarily dazzled him.

"It's looking better already," said Byte.

Jake smiled. "Yeah. At least it's starting to *look* like something a real musician would own. Now we hope that the wood hasn't dried out too much and that all the pads have tight seals."

He rubbed some oil into the wood, and the teak took on a rich gloss. The clarinet finally looked as it should— like a very old, very fine musical instrument.

"Well, come on," said Peter. "Let's hear it."

It was time for the test. Jake joined the two halves of the instrument's barrel, added the bell, then fitted the mouthpiece into place. The ligature on the mouthpiece was old and rusty, so Jake replaced it with a shiny new one. Lastly, he took one of his best Vandoren #4 reeds, placed it in the mouthpiece, and secured it with the ligature.

Then Jake closed his eyes and brought the clarinet to his lips.

He stopped suddenly when the first note sounded. The century-old wood vibrated with a richness that no new clarinet, not even the one in Garlick's window, could emulate. Jake stared at the instrument, his fingers tingling, and he noticed that his friends sat with their mouths open. A moment passed before one of them finally spoke.

"Jake," Byte said quietly, "that was absolutely beautiful."

"So does that mean it's not a piece of junk?" Mattie asked.

Peter smiled. "Hey, I didn't know you were that good," he teased.

Jake continued to play. In the low ranges, the clarinet sounded full and rich. At the high end, the tone was sweet and carried no hint of the squeal he sometimes heard in his composite instrument.

And yet something about the clarinet bothered him. Jake's ear had picked up a problem. Behind every rich note, the clarinet made a light buzzing sound, barely audible, like a mosquito flying on the other side of the room. He stopped playing and looked at the others. "Do you hear that?" he asked. "That weird—I don't know—vibration or something?"

Jake frowned, and he pulled the clarinet apart to see if he could find what was causing the noise. At first he saw nothing. But when he looked more closely, he saw something sticking out beyond the edge of the barrel. When he pulled at it, it came out slowly, crinkling in his fingers.

It was a small slip of paper, dry and yellowed, and it bore someone's scribbled handwriting. Only the scrawled words "love, Growler" were immediately clear.

Peter moved to stare over Jake's left shoulder. "What is it?" he asked.

"I don't know," said Jake, reading and shrugging. "It's some kind of note. But it doesn't make any sense."

Byte and Mattie came closer to see the paper as well. Jake passed the note to Mattie.

"Look," said Mattie, "it's signed by Growler himself."

Jake had his lips on the instrument again, but Mattie's comment made him freeze. "Hey," he said, "that's right." He looked down at his instrument. "Who knows? Maybe this clarinet was one of Growler Morton's favorites. Maybe he used it on some famous recording." Jake smiled at the others. "Wow, I might own a piece of jazz history here."

"Before the auction, had you ever heard of Growler Morton?" asked Mattie.

Jake paused. "Well, okay, so maybe it's not really *important* history."

"I can hardly read this note," said Byte. "What does it say… 'One must look in the twenty-third place'? What's that supposed to mean?"

Mattie's face brightened. "Hey, maybe Growler Morton wanted somebody to find that and figure out what it means," he said.

"Hey," echoed Peter, "*maybe* it's a reminder of where he left his car keys." When he saw Mattie's disappointed expression, he plucked a card from the center of the scattered deck. "Okay, how about you show me that trick?"

Jake placed the clarinet to his lips once again. While Mattie attempted to astonish Peter and Byte with his card trick, Jake blew a jazz riff that started high, then wandered down to a bluesy low. The last note echoed— a long, lonely, windlike moan.

In a hotel room in downtown Bugle Point, Karl Logan opened a leather briefcase and began setting up his temporary office. The first item he looked at was the fax he had received from his client. As promised, it was a typed description of the items he was to acquire, along with the time and location of the auction. Beneath this letter, made even more grainy by the faxing process, was a 1957 newspaper photograph of the items themselves: a clarinet, an old 45-rpm record, and some pieces of sheet music.

Logan put the fax aside and reached for the rest of his work. He removed a stack of 8x10 black-and-white photographs, and he studied them until he could visualize them with his eyes closed. They were photographs of this morning's auction at the Morton home. During the auction, Logan had parked his black van a full block down the street. He had photographed the auction with a Nikon 35mm camera and a 1000mm telescopic lens, 3200 ISO high-speed film, and a 2X extender. Now he viewed the clear, close-up pictures he had taken of his subjects. He knew exactly which items had sold, and he had memorized the faces of the people who had made the purchases.

Now he only had to attach names to those faces, and his job was all but finished.

He reached into the case again and removed a small laptop computer. Then he removed the cord from the

hotel room phone and plugged it into the computer's modem jack.

Logan had arrived in Bugle Point last Friday morning. Friday night he had scouted the offices of Starlight Auctions. The offices, he discovered, lay on the second floor of a three-story office building just outside the downtown area of Bugle Point. The ground entrance faced the street and had an alarm system that, though pitifully inadequate, nonetheless led Karl to the conclusion that a rooftop approach would be simpler. With the help of an awning and an iron railing attached to the balcony of an apartment next door, Karl made it to the building's roof. From there he rappelled down the rear of the building to a second-story window.

A child could have gotten through the window itself.

The computer system was password secure, but Karl did not have need of the computer—at least, not yet. What he had come for was information, information that would allow him access to the computer files later, after the Morton auction. The system would likely require both a user name and password. Karl looked first for a name. Simple: The secretary's desk was drowned in paper, each sheet covered with tiny Post-it notes leaving instructions for someone named Debbie.

Karl then examined every item on Debbie's desk— overturning the Rolodex, lifting the blotter, rifling through the stacks of paper, checking both the handset

36 and base of the telephone, searching for Debbie's password into the computer system. A new secretary would write it down somewhere, and once memorized, the password might remain, forgotten, in its hiding place. He found it taped to the underside of a desk drawer, a Starlight business card with the word "going1nce" scrawled hastily on the obverse side.

Logan, after making certain he had left everything as he had found it, slipped back out through the window, closing it carefully as he left. Any thief could break into a building, he reminded himself. Only the best could break in, get what he wanted, and leave without anyone ever knowing he'd been there.

Now that the auction was over and Logan was comfortable in a hotel room, ready to go to work, he dialed into Starlight's system. When it came time to type in an access code, he entered Debbie's. In seconds Karl Logan had access to Starlight's files. He located the file marked "Morton," and there, right at his fingertips, was the name and address of every person who had made a purchase at the Morton auction.

Logan studied the file. There was McCollum, the antique dealer. Logan would deal with him soon enough. *But*, he thought, *first things first.* The easier target, he decided, would be the boy. Logan scrolled through the file until he located the purchaser of the clarinet.

There it was.

He leaned back in his chair and watched the boy's name and address flicker in the center of his computer screen. *Yes*, he thought. *McCollum will come later.*

His first target would be the teenager—Jake Armstrong.

chapter
three

Monday

On Monday morning, Jake lay in bed and gazed at his new clarinet, his hands crossed behind his head and a dim, sleepy smile on his face. A bebop solo, full of crackling notes—sixteen to a measure—tittered through his mind.

After he hit the snooze button on his alarm clock three times, he finally dragged himself from bed. Jake showered, dressed, and tugged on a pair of socks, only to pull them off a moment later when he discovered that one was black and the other navy blue. He lost another five minutes searching for his homework, which he found amid some jazz scribblings he had left on his music stand. He knew he had worn jeans yesterday, but he could not remember which pair, so he searched the pockets of all three until he located his car keys. Through it all, the bebop number sang in his head.

Jake and his parents lived in one of the outlying areas of Bugle Point. Living that far out gave the family lots of space and trees and fresh air, but it also meant that Jake had a long drive into town.

He strode to his car, his feet scuffing the gravel, and threw his schoolbooks, notebook, and lunch. He carefully placed the clarinet on the passenger seat. The Escort rumbled and jittered while Jake let the engine warm. The jittering didn't stop until he guided the shift through first and second, and, finally, into third gear.

Jake had to travel a narrow, two-lane road for several miles until he came to a stop sign, and from there another two miles until he arrived at school. More often than not Jake enjoyed the drive, but today a battered green Cadillac pulled in behind him. It shot out from a small side road and accelerated until it trailed just a few feet behind the Escort. Jake found himself glaring into his rearview mirror.

A couple of miles later, when the two cars approached the stop sign, Jake slowed, and the Cadillac, too close for safety, tapped the rear end of Jake's car. The impact threw Jake forward in his seat so that the seatbelt harness caught him and yanked him back.

Jake put the car in park and turned off the engine with a sigh. *I do not need this,* he told himself. He reached for his wallet, his registration, and his proof of insurance. Stepping from his car, Jake knelt beside the rear bumper and surveyed the damage. He spied a small dent, but, considering the condition of the rest of the car, it was unlikely that anyone but Jake would notice. He motioned to the man in the Cadillac to pull over, then climbed back in and maneuvered his car onto the shoulder.

Now that he was safe from the occasional car speeding past, Jake turned his attention to the man sitting in the Cadillac. The driver was an elderly man wearing a baggy plaid shirt, suspenders, and a black bolo tie with a turquoise fastener. He was rummaging through the Cadillac's glove compartment. He brought out some papers, flipped through them, then tossed them aside. Then, just as Jake reached the window of the car, the man yanked down the sun visor. A slip of paper, probably the car's registration, fluttered down into the man's lap. He gathered it up and stepped out of the car.

"Sorry, son," he said in a faint Southern accent, his old voice wavering. "Guess this one's my fault." He looked past Jake's shoulder at the fresh dent in the Escort, and his face fell. "Oh, dear," he said, "did I do that?"

Jake nodded and reached for the man's paperwork. "I'm afraid so."

The man scratched at his bulbous nose. "Well, I declare." He was tall, almost as tall as Jake, but his shoulders were bent and rolled forward, as with age. His skin, like that of a farmer or construction worker, was tanned and leathery. "Been driving almost fifty years," said the man, "and never had an accident. That's what I get for bird watching." He smiled and pointed to the top branches of an oak tree that lay off to the side of the road. "A Western tanager took off from those branches and flew like a bandit across that field there. Did you see it?"

"No, I missed that," said Jake. "Look, sir, I don't mean to be rude, but do you think we could do this quickly? I'm running late enough as it is." He was jotting down as much information as he could—the man's name, Walter Gleason, his address, and the number off his driver's license. He also wrote down the license number of the Cadillac and the name and phone number of Walter Gleason's insurance agent. He offered his own paperwork to the man, but Mr. Gleason just waved it off.

"Don't need all that," he said. "I'm fairly sure you'll be getting in touch with me."

Jake nodded and handed back the man's paperwork, grateful that the incident wasn't going to make him late for school. He turned and headed toward his car.

"Young man," Mr. Gleason called, "may I ask you a favor?" He looked hopefully at Jake.

Jake hesitated. Gleason was pleasant enough, but that fact had not yet wiped away Jake's annoyance with the fender bender.

"I'm sorry," Mr. Gleason said. "I don't want to put you out." He started to get back into his car.

"No, it's fine," said Jake finally. "What can I help you with?"

The man grinned, and he clapped his hands together. He moved quickly to the driver's side door of his car, reached through the open window, and yanked the hood

42 release. The hood popped up an inch, and for the first time Jake noticed the black smoke trailing from underneath. The old man looked at Jake and smiled, his face tinged with embarrassment.

"Somethin' wrong with the buggy here," he said, shrugging his shoulders. "I never learned anything about cars. Think you could take a moment to look at it? I'm afraid the engine'll burn up before I even get home."

Jake took in a deep breath and let it out slowly. The old guy wrung his hands, waiting for an answer. It looked like Jake was going to be a few minutes late for school after all. "All right," Jake said, "not a problem."

He reached under the Cadillac's grill and released the latch. As Jake pulled up the hood, its rusty hinges squealed. Black smoke stung Jake's nostrils. He squinted. Jake knew a little about cars, but the smoke seemed to be coming from the engine, which meant the problem— whatever it might be—was way out of Jake's league.

Mr. Gleason stepped away from the car, focusing on some chittering bird noises in a nearby tree. *At least he won't be staring over my shoulder*, thought Jake.

Jake had seen smoke pouring from a car's exhaust, but he had never seen it trailing off an engine like this. And the smell! Jake breathed shallowly, frowning. The surface of the engine was glossy, covered with a gritty shine. *Oil.* Surely oil shouldn't be all over a hot engine. Did that mean a leak? Jake wasn't sure, but this burning oil definitely signified some major problem.

"Hey," said Jake. "I don't know how it got here, but you've got oil burning all over the surface of this engine."

He looked up from the car, searching for Mr. Gleason, wanting to make sure the old man had heard him.

Gleason stood several feet away, his mouth a grim line. Behind him was Jake's Escort, the driver's side door gaping open. "Well," said Mr. Gleason, "you figured that out very quickly."

Jake looked first at the old man, then at his car, then at the old man, struggling to put together what he was seeing. "What?…"

He took a step toward Mr. Gleason, inadvertently placing himself between the old man and the driver's side door of the Cadillac. The old man also moved toward Jake—he was fast, very fast—and the heel of the man's hand smacked the side of Jake's nose before Jake saw the blow coming. His body spun from the impact, and he landed in the dirt.

In a flicker of movement, the old man slipped back into the Cadillac and cranked the engine. The car roared, and Jake rolled away from the sound. His temple throbbed. Drops of blood fell from his nostrils and spotted the ground in front of him.

Gleason whipped the Caddy around like a Hollywood stunt driver, the car spitting up gravel as it left. The old man was out of sight before the teenager even had a chance to wipe the dust from his eyes.

Jake struggled to his feet and staggered to his car. He looked down the road where the Cadillac had disappeared, still stunned by the viciousness of the blow to his head. He dragged his shirtsleeve across the bottom of his nose, wiping away the blood, and examined the

44   inside of his car. His bagged lunch still lay on the passenger seat. His schoolbooks were scattered on the floor behind the driver's seat. Everything was just as he had left it.

Everything except…

Jake doubled over as though the old man had hit him a second time. He turned around, his back leaning against the car, and he slid to the ground until his legs folded and his fingers dabbed lightly against his tender, swelling nose. He closed his eyes and remained seated in the dust for several minutes, thinking back on what had just happened and trying to make sense of it.

The old man had stolen his clarinet.

Walter Gleason was five miles away when he pulled the Cadillac off the road and drove it into a clearing in the woods. He parked it next to a black van.

Moving with the grace of a much younger man, he scrambled into the van and studied himself in the rearview mirror. He scratched at his bulbous nose. He scratched, and he pulled at his skin, until a seam formed—right where the bottom of his nose rounded into his upper lip. He scratched some more, and the seam widened. He worked at the seam until he was able to dig his finger underneath it.

Then he tore the nose right off his face.

The nose, which was made of latex foam, went into a case that served as a professional disguise kit. In the kit were several other noses, three different types of ears, tinted contact lenses of every shade, makeup for altering skin color, hair dyes, wigs and hair extensions, and an assortment of prosthetics for creating lifelike wrinkles and scars.

After putting the nose away in its proper compartment, Gleason clawed at his forehead until he created a seam there as well. When he pulled, the wrinkled forehead—and the skullcap with its thinning hair—peeled off in one piece. Underneath was the short brown hair and fair skin of Karl Logan.

Not your best, Logan, he thought, disgusted. *You had to hit the kid.* Karl Logan took it as a personal failing whenever he had to use violence. He locked up the disguise kit, placing it in the van's rear compartment.

Step one was finished.

Jake sat, angry and sullen, through his first-period jazz band class. He had had to borrow a clarinet—a *composition* clarinet—from Mr. Janson, the band director. He said nothing about losing his own. A couple of the other band members stared at the deep, blue-green bruise across his nose and cheekbones, concerned. Patty Arbour, the freshman girl who played second clarinet— and who had to tug off her retainer each time she played—handed Jake a note that said "Everything all right?" Patty had dotted the *I*s with tiny scrawled hearts. Jake smiled at her and shook his head.

46   During a break, Jake tore three sheets of paper from his notebook and withdrew to a chair in the back of the room.

He scribbled a quick note on each sheet of paper, then folded the sheets and marked them with an emblem, a circle superimposed over a square. It was the symbol Jake and his friends had adopted for their group: symbols for a square peg and a round hole. These simple geometric figures spoke to Jake in a very personal way. They were like wooden puzzle pieces that overlapped without fitting together. Like Jake and his friends, they were misfits.

Jake would give the notes to Mattie Ramiro. Mattie had an almost supernatural ability for locating and homing in on the others. Jake could give Mattie the messages and relax, knowing that Peter Braddock and Byte Salzmann, wherever they were, would have the notes in their hands before the start of the next class period.

Byte left her first-period trig class and headed across campus. Her next class, biology, was all the way in the D wing, and she would need the full five-minute passing period to get there.

Today she had tied her wavy, dark blond hair into a ponytail, which swung between her shoulders as she walked. A lengthy search through her closet this morning had produced a blue and red and black tie-dyed T-shirt, a pair of lavender jeans that flared at the ankle, and, because it was a little cool today, her black imitation leather jacket with the fringe dangling across the front and down the sleeves. She crinkled her nose, hitching up her wire-framed granny glasses.

Perhaps because of the lavender bell-bottoms, or the *Earth First!* button pinned to her shirt, or the computer bag that slapped against her thigh as she walked, other students threw odd looks at her as she passed. Byte ignored them, skittering by without speaking and without looking back. *Let them stare*, she thought. Today those stares, and the sinking feeling they usually left in her stomach, fled away under the sun and the knowledge that she would soon be with her friends.

She was especially looking forward to seeing Jake. He had been so distracted and quiet since he hadn't made soloist in the band—and silence was his way, Byte knew, of expressing unhappiness. But now she knew how thrilled he was about his new clarinet, and she wanted to hear about his first practice. The clarinet meant so much to him.

Mattie was waiting for her in the usual place. Because it was the morning break time, he was seated outside on one of the school's wide, concrete benches, and he had spread out the contents of his pockets as though he were in his own private laboratory. As she neared him, Byte watched him work. He had his multi-tool in his hand, and he was fiddling with a tiny box made of black plastic. Mattie had laid the box open for surgery, exposing several wires that led to a series of little green lights.

"Hi," said Byte. "What are you doing?"

Mattie fumbled with the box before answering. "Um—*ouch!*—I'm messing with Jake's tuner. Had algebra work to do last night, so I'm just now getting to it." He held the box up, showing it to Byte. "See? Jake's supposed to be able to play a note, and the little lights tell him whether he's sharp or flat. Jake can't get it to work right, remember?" Mattie used the screwdriver on his multi-tool to pry up a metal connection inside the battery compartment. "Ah, so I was right. See? This connection is just loose. Makes the battery slip, then it loses contact and the power goes off. I'll just bend it up a little so it makes better contact."

"Nice work," said Byte. "That'll make Jake happy."

"I am the wizard," said Mattie. He wiggled his fingers as though casting a spell on the tiny digital device. When he tightened the screws and snapped shut the battery compartment, the green lights flickered.

As he was putting away his multi-tool, a tiny freshman girl with a huge mass of strawberry blond curls stepped away from her group of friends. She approached Mattie, glancing over her shoulder at her friends before greeting him. "Hi," she said.

"Oh hi, Caitlyn," Mattie replied.

"Do you have it?" she asked.

Mattie reached into his coat pocket, took out an electronic organizer, and handed it to the girl. "All done," he said.

"Cool. What do I owe you?"

Mattie shrugged. "Five bucks. The circuit board was cracked. Still is, but I re-soldered the connection. Should work fine if you don't drop it again."

"Hey, you're so awesome!"

Mattie beamed. The girl reached into her bag for a five-dollar bill and handed it to him. She then opened up the organizer, pressed the power button, and began scrolling through the instrument's calendar. "Oh, *no*," she cried, "I forgot about the math club meeting!" She dashed off, yelling a loud thanks to Mattie as she left.

Byte shook her head and grinned. "What's next?" she asked. "Written warranties on parts and labor?"

"Hey," said Mattie, "that's not a bad idea."

He reached into his shirt pocket and took out three folded notes. Each bore the circle/square emblem of Misfits, Inc., the name Peter had given their group. Mattie held the notes in his fingers, fanning them like a hand of playing cards. The center one bore Byte's name.

"It's bad news," he said.

Byte stared at Mattie, waiting and hoping for some sign that he was joking, but no sign came. She reached for the center note and tugged it from Mattie's fingers. "Bad news?" she repeated.

Mattie nodded gravely. "It's all there," he said, glancing at her watch. "Can't talk anymore. I have to find Peter."

Mattie picked up his belongings and ran off, vanishing into a crowd of students in that peculiar way he had. Byte found herself struggling to unfold the sheet of

50 paper. Finally she managed to open it, tearing one corner in the process, and she read the note as she hurried to her next class.

Byte recognized the handwriting immediately. She smiled, even as she felt a touch of disappointment. The note was from Jake. She had the fleeting thought that it would be nice, just once, to get a note from Jake that wasn't also intended for every other member of the group—a friendly message, just between Jake and Byte.

But that thought faded when she finished reading the note. Byte stopped walking, closed her eyes, and crumpled the sheet of paper in her fingers. *Oh, no,* she thought, *Jake's just going to die...*

Peter Braddock strode from his chemistry class, his spine tingling and his face warm with embarrassment. He had only wanted to *help*. He knew some of the other students were struggling; he had seen their frustration in the way they slammed their textbooks shut at the end of the period, or the way they huddled together, asking desperate questions when they thought Mr. Blair wasn't looking.

So today, when Mr. Blair left the classroom to photocopy some extra handouts, Peter saw an opportunity to help these students—and perhaps to make some new friends in the process. Most were too shy to ask questions, so Peter decided to stand up in front of the class and continue the lesson where Mr. Blair left off.

He started by picking up the chalk from the chalk tray and tossing it toward the ceiling, hoping to snatch it from the air as it dropped. Instead, it bounced off his palm, struck the floor, and broke into half a dozen pieces. Peter picked up the largest fragment—it was about the size of a jellybean—and tried to write with it. As he did, his fingernail squealed against the chalkboard.

"Oh, God, here it comes," said a student.

"Siddown," called another.

"Listen," Peter said, "let's talk a little about this concept of isotopes."

"He's doing an impression of Mr. Blair!" one girl in the back hissed.

A few students tittered.

"One classic example would be deuterium," Peter went on, "otherwise known as heavy hydrogen." He drew a diagram on the board with his tiny piece of chalk, showing how the deuterium atom had twice the atomic weight of normal hydrogen.

At first, few students paid any attention. But moments later, as Peter warmed to the subject, he was sure he was winning them over. A few began staring, their mouths open. Many looked hard at him, showing their first taste of genuine understanding. Peter felt a warmth of satisfaction. It felt *good* to help others.

That thought lasted until the paper airplane bounced off Peter's nose.

"Siddown," repeated the voice, "and shuddup." And when Peter did, the classroom burst into applause.

Now he walked red faced to his English class, paying scant attention to the corridor full of people around him. His mind reviewed what had happened: He understood the material; that much was certain. He had presented it clearly. Indeed, he had offered his own insights for the benefit of the entire class. So why had they reacted the way they did?

Peter continued to ponder, the world a blur around him, until he felt a finger tapping on his shoulder. He turned and saw Mattie. The younger boy was holding a folded slip of notebook paper that bore the Misfits' emblem.

Peter saw the look on Mattie's face. "Trouble, huh?" he said. He took the folded note and stuck it into his shirt pocket. "Is Jake okay?"

Mattie shrugged. "Doubt it," he said. "Read the note. Or read my mind." He smiled. "We'll talk later."

Peter suppressed a grin. At least someone appreciated his brain.

"Bell's going to ring," said Mattie. "Gotta go."

Mattie turned and left. Peter touched the note in his pocket and thought about what it might contain. He did not know for sure, but Mattie's expression and Jake's scratchy version of the Misfits' emblem had told him much already.

Peter opened the note, and his eyes widened. *How? Why?* he wondered.

The note asked the Misfits to meet after school.

After that, they would visit the Bugle Point Police Department.

Bugle Point P.D. Robbery Division 4:00 p.m.

Lieutenant Marvin Decker sat at his desk, hunched over a newspaper. He was poring through the arts and entertainment section. His wife had asked for tickets to the ballet, and the only way to surprise her was to order the tickets from work. He flipped through page after page, desperate to find the information and order tickets before his partner, Sam, returned and caught on to what he was doing. Sadly, the newspaper wasn't much help.

So, he wondered, staring at an advertisement for a monster truck show, *where's the pictures of the guys in tights?*

His stomach growled. Decker reached for the small bowl of carrot sticks that lay on the corner of his desktop—another of his wife's ideas. He picked up a single stick and stared at it, as if by so doing he could turn it into a bag of Chee-tos. When he bit into it, the carrot made an angry cracking sound between his teeth.

Sam walked into the office carrying a sheaf of papers. The newspaper rustled as Decker quickly folded it and tossed it on a corner of his desktop. When Sam turned toward the sound, Decker gazed downward, as though the file in front of him would lead to the capture of every villain on the FBI's Most Wanted list. He was *busy,* darn it! He wanted Sam to see that.

54   The sheaf of papers landed with a smack on Decker's desk. "Here's the completed report on that series of convenience store holdups," said Sam.

"Great," said Decker.

Sam pointed to the folded newspaper. "That the entertainment section?"

"Sports," muttered Decker. "Haven't you got anything to do?"

Just then Decker heard voices outside the office doorway. Four teenagers entered, and Decker recognized them instantly. It was those kids, the ones who seemed to have their noses stuck in every bizarre case that came Decker's way. He chewed the last of his carrot and folded his arms across his chest. "Well, well," he said, "what can I do for you?"

Decker expected the leader of the group, the Braddock kid, to step forward. He was surprised when the big kid, the one called Jake, took charge instead. He was less surprised when he saw the blue-black bruise that spread across Jake's nose and cheekbones.

"Lieutenant," said Jake, "I would like to report a theft."

Decker listened as Jake related the story of the clarinet purchase, the message from Growler, the automobile accident, and the theft of the clarinet. Decker was clearly more interested in the theft than he was in a forty-year-old slip of paper. He tapped his finger against his lip as Jake described the old man. He glanced at the slip of paper on which Jake had written the man's name, address, and license information.

"Sorry about your horn, kid," Decker said. "But look, this is Robbery Division, okay? The uniforms handle petty theft. Why don't you take this information to the officer at the desk, and she'll help you write up a report."

None of the teens budged. *Why*, Decker asked himself, *am I not surprised?*

"Lieutenant," said the Braddock kid, "after all the help we've given you? Remember that valuable computer chip we helped *you* recover? The black market video pirates we helped *you* capture? Didn't you get a commendation in one of those cases?"

Decker sighed and took the slip of paper. "Awright, awright," he said, handing it to Sam. "Run a DMV check on this, okay? See what comes up."

Then the lieutenant looked at Jake. "This guy must be a regular Einstein. He practically gives you his whole life story—everything we need to just knock on his door and arrest him—and then he's stupid enough to steal your clarinet." He leaned back in his chair. "Don't worry, kid," he said. "We'll get your horn back."

Moments later Sam returned. He was holding a computer printout in his hand, and his face was blank. "Here's the information you asked for," he said. He looked at Jake, then at Decker. "A Cadillac with that license number was stolen last night…from the police impound lot."

"*Our* impound lot?" asked Decker, incredulous. "This guy's got guts—or he's crazy. What about the driver's license?"

56 Sam's mouth tightened. "That's the funny part," he said. "The license number and name check out, but there's a problem."

"And that is?" said Decker.

Sam took a deep breath. "Walter Gleason is not an old man." He looked at Jake. "He's a nineteen year old. And his registered vehicle is a Kawasaki motorcycle."

Forty minutes later the Misfits gathered in Jake's bedroom. Jake sat on the floor, his back to the wall. The composition clarinet his parents had bought for him when he was in middle school lay in pieces at his feet. He was trying to assemble the instrument, but the bell didn't seem to fit; Jake—absorbed by thoughts of the theft and of Walter Gleason—had forgotten to properly grease the cork. He gripped the bell, twisting it back and forth to force it on, and the frustration within him grew. Suddenly he heard a *crack*—like a booted foot stepping on a large twig—and felt a momentary vibration in his hand. When he looked down, he saw a four-inch split in the clarinet's barrel.

He tossed the barrel onto his bed and rubbed his eyes. "Why would that old guy want my clarinet?" he wondered aloud.

Byte wandered across the room and sat down next to him. "He probably saw it in your car and just took it," she said quietly. "It may be as simple as that."

"Doubtful," said Peter. He straddled Jake's desk chair, frowning. "Remember, he didn't just casually swipe something valuable. The old man had false ID and was driving a stolen car. He went to a great deal of trouble to get the clarinet, hit Jake when he got in his way, then took off."

"What are you saying, that the fender bender and theft were planned?" asked Byte. She looked at Jake. "No offense. It was a nice clarinet. But to go to that much trouble to steal it? That's a little weird, don't you think? Besides, this Gleason guy couldn't have known you even *had* a clarinet."

Mattie sat on the edge of Jake's desk, balancing a pencil on the tip of his nose. "The old man is definitely senile. That's the only explanation."

"I don't think he was crazy," Peter insisted. "He'd gotten away with a lot already—stealing the car from the police impound lot and creating a convincing fake ID. He must have known that Jake would report the accident and find out he wasn't who he said he was. To me all of his actions suggest confidence—maybe even arrogance. It's like he doesn't care what the police find out, because he figures they can't catch him anyway."

With that, the four grew silent. Jake understood all too well what Peter was saying. If the old man was so unafraid of the police that he would dare *play* with them by stealing a car from their own impound lot and providing false identification for them to track, then there was no telling what he might have done to Jake to get what he wanted.

"Okay," Mattie said, "if we assume he *did* set out to steal the clarinet—"

58 "Wait. If he *did* really set out to steal it," Byte said, "that means he knew where Jake was, and he knew Jake would have the clarinet with him—which would mean he'd been following Jake!"

"But why would he go to so much trouble?" Jake asked, shaking his head. "I just don't get it. It makes no *sense*. It was just a beat-up old clarinet." He rose slowly and walked to his desk, mentally ticking off the strange aspects of the theft: the way the old man had set up fake damage to the Cadillac's engine by pouring oil over the red-hot engine block, the way he had moved just before striking Jake, like an athlete or dancer. What sort of man was this? And what was so important about an antique clarinet? As his thoughts wandered, his eyes happened to fall to his desktop. Growler Morton's note was still resting beneath the stapler.

"Hey," said Jake. "*Hey*...maybe the guy was looking for something else."

"You mean the note?" Byte asked. "'One must look in the twenty-third place'?"

Jake shrugged. "It makes as much sense as anything else."

Peter nodded. "It's an interesting possibility," he said. Then he looked at Byte. "What can we find out about this Growler Morton?"

Byte reached for the bag containing her laptop computer. "I'm on it," she said.

In a few moments, she had connected Jake's phone line to her modem jack and booted up her system. She waited a moment, then keyed in a phone number. Mattie scooted next to her to watch.

"That's not your online provider," he said.

Byte nodded. "Right," she said. "I'm trying something a little different." The computer quietly whirred, and the screen resolved into a picture of the logo for the *Bugle Point Courier,* the city's largest newspaper. "One of my mom's friends," said Byte, "works for the paper. Mom knew I was struggling with a report on water pollution, so she asked her friend to give me the modem number for the paper's morgue."

"Morgue?" asked Jake.

Byte was silent for a moment while she keyed in some commands. "Um, yeah. It's kind of a graveyard for old newspaper stories. The paper used to keep all its old stories in hard copy files, in case reporters needed to look up something. You know, like when an event took place or when a certain robbery happened. Now they've taken all those files and put them on CD-ROM, and people like me can access them via the Internet."

Mattie nodded. "Cool. So you can type in a person's name, then look up any newspaper story that was ever written about that person?"

Byte smiled. "You got it."

She typed in "Morton, Growler," and a menu listing five stories appeared. Several appeared to be notices of upcoming jazz performances. One looked like a critic's review of a performance.

Byte picked the one labeled **Disappearance of...**

60   The newspaper's logo vanished, replaced by a blurry photograph of a handsome young black man. He was wearing a white tuxedo with a carnation in the lapel, and his eyes were closed as he blew into a clarinet. The headline of the article proclaimed "Jazz Musician Sought in Theft."

August 14, 1957

Police are seeking jazz clarinetist Jerome "Growler" Morton for questioning in the theft of $3,000,000 from the musician's recording label. Morton disappeared last week, just days before RSA Records executives reported that $3,000,000 worth of negotiable bearer bonds were missing from the company safe. Franklin Bellows, a vice president at RSA, said, "I knew Growler was having some problems, but I never dreamed he'd resort to this. He was more than just a musician under contract here. He was my friend."

Morton, 28, was a virtual unknown until two years ago, when his recording "Whisper My Name" went to the top of the charts...

The article went on to list Growler Morton's musical accomplishments. Jake read it over Byte's shoulder, but it didn't seem to offer much useful information.

"Okay," said Mattie, "so about forty years ago this jerk swiped beaucoup bucks from his record label. So what does that have to do with Jake or the clarinet or the old man or the note?"

"The article doesn't say that Morton was guilty," Peter cautioned. "Just that he was wanted for questioning. We've been looking for a reason why an old man would steal a car, make a fake ID, and steal a clarinet. Three million dollars, if it's still floating around out there somewhere, could explain a lot."

Byte was shaking her head. "It doesn't make sense," she said. "If these bonds or whatever were stolen forty years ago, why would it matter now?" She continued scrolling through articles on Morton. "I mean, whoever stole these bonds must have cashed them and spent the money long ago. Nobody steals three million bucks unless they're planning to spend it."

"That's what they would be hoping to do," said Peter, "but who knows? 'Best laid plans' and all that."

"Right," said Mattie. "Maybe this Growler Morton guy took the money, hid it, then died *before* he could spend it." He smiled broadly. "Hey, if we can solve this case, we might be millionaires!"

"Right, Mattie," Byte said. "And if you lose a tooth this afternoon, you might find the missing bonds under your pillow tomorrow morning."

"You never know." Mattie grinned at her, obviously pleased with himself.

Byte rolled her eyes.

Jake wandered over to his window and stared out into his front yard. Beyond a small group of fruit trees lay the two-lane road that took Jake to town. Somewhere in the distance was the stop sign where "Walter Gleason" had rammed Jake's car and stolen the clarinet.

What happened forty years ago was irrelevant, Jake thought; the theft of his clarinet had made this a very personal matter—and a matter for the present.

"All right," Peter said. "We have two places to start—"

"Right," Jake said, turning to face the others. "We need to talk to Helen Morton, and we need to pay a visit to RSA Records."

chapter
four

Tuesday

When school ended Tuesday, Jake and Byte drove to the Morton home. Jake remained silent during the entire trip, his mind focused on the old man and the stolen clarinet. A voice inside Jake whispered that Peter was the wisest of the group, that Peter should be the one asking questions and controlling the investigation. But another voice, a louder voice, reminded Jake that the responsibility was his, and this thought weighed heavily on his mind. Once or twice Byte looked over at him, but instead of speaking she finally just reached into the glove compartment, selected one of Jake's favorite jazz CDs, and slipped it into the car stereo.

He guided his Escort past a For Sale sign and down the long cobblestone drive that led to Helen Morton's home. Byte turned toward him, finally voicing her thoughts. "Are you all right?"

Jake nodded, silent.

64   Two days ago, when its furnishings were cast out for auction on the back lawn, and the table of refreshments lay adorned with fruit and tiny sandwiches, and all the antique buyers milled about, chatting, the Morton home had bustled with activity. Today, however, the house seemed small, modest, and even a little sad. The auction had apparently been a prelude to a move. The curtains were gone, leaving empty windows whose glass shone almost black in the bright sun. Now the only bustle came from the painters who worked their brushes along the home's exterior.

Jake and Byte walked up a stone path to the front porch. Once there, they paused at a set of oak doors decorated with stained glass. Jake took a deep breath, looked at Byte, and knocked.

"I'm not even sure I know what to say," he told her.

"You'll do fine," Byte answered. She gave him a reassuring smile.

Distant voices came from within the house, but no one answered the door. Jake and Byte waited several seconds, and both felt a growing discomfort until finally the lock turned, the door opened a crack, and a man's face peered out. He was black and appeared to be around forty. The man was pleasant looking, but Jake noticed a wariness in the man's eyes. He studied Jake and Byte for a long moment before speaking.

"What do you want?" he demanded.

Jake threw a quick glance at Byte. He handed the man a business card.

misfits inc.
investigations

Mysteries are no mystery to us!

Jake Armstrong   Matthew Ramiro
Peter Braddock   Byte Salzmann

"Excuse me," said Jake. "My name is Jake Armstrong. This is my friend, Byte Salzmann. We were wondering if we could talk to Mrs. Morton."

The man continued to study them, noticing in particular the laptop computer nestled in the bag at Byte's shoulder. "Mrs. Morton," he said, "is very busy. She doesn't have time for casual chats or interviews." His dark eyes glared at them. "And," he added, "if you're here because you're fans of Growler Morton, and you think you're going to intrude on our privacy just so you can 'bathe in his vibrations' or catch his image in a 'spirit photograph' or some such nonsense, you can forget it. I'll call the police and have you escorted from the property right now."

"Um, we're not here for any of those things," said Jake. "We just wanted to talk to Mrs. Morton about this...."

He reached into his coat pocket and withdrew Growler Morton's note, which he had slipped into a plastic bag for protection. He passed it to the man, hoping with all his might that the man wouldn't just shred the note into bits of confetti. He needn't have worried. The man squinted at the writing, and his features softened.

"Where did you get this?" he asked softly.

"I was at the auction the other day," replied Jake. "It was inside the clarinet I bought."

The man looked at Jake, then at Byte. "Wait here," he said. "I'll be back in a moment." The door shut rather abruptly in Jake's face. Moments later, when the man returned, he opened the door wide and stepped aside so Jake and Byte could enter. "Mother says she'll see you," he told them. "But she's very tired. You have five minutes."

He led them through a living room and down a long hallway, his rubber-soled sneakers squeaking against the marble floor. The walls, Jake noticed, were the same light-colored wood as the front door—tongue-and-groove planks of solid oak.

"Nice place," whispered Byte. "Think it's worth three million dollars?"

Jake raised an eyebrow but said nothing.

They entered what appeared to be a den or library. In it was a television set, a baby grand piano, an expensive stereo system, and a wooden floor unit holding dozens of CDs. One wall accommodated a window, but floor-to-ceiling bookshelves lined the other three. The shelves were half-empty. Most of the books were stacked in cardboard boxes that lay scattered here and there across

the carpet. Crumpled sheets of butcher paper and ker-
nels of Styrofoam popcorn littered the floor.

In the center of the mess stood a striking woman.
Helen Morton was a black woman in her early sixties.
She was not beautiful—at least not in a glamorous
way—but she did have an almost indescribable dignity.
She was wearing blue jeans and an untucked long sleeve
blouse that fell to her hips, but the squareness to her
shoulders and straightness of her back commanded
respect.

"Hello," she said, and she dusted little flecks of
Styrofoam from her fingers. "I'm Helen Morton. And
you two have certainly got my attention." She walked
over and shook Jake's hand, then Byte's, as they introduced themselves.

The man who had led them to the room handed
Growler Morton's note back to Jake, then raised his
index finger as a warning. His features once more took
on a hard and angry look. "Five minutes," he commanded. Then he strode from the room.

Helen Morton watched the man leave, and she smiled
apologetically at Jake and Byte. "That's my son, Scott,"
she said. "You'll have to pardon him. The auction has
brought my late husband back into the news, and we've
been deluged with calls. Every tabloid wants an interview. Lots of—well, let's just say 'eccentric'—people have
been knocking at the door. It's been exhausting."

"We'll try not to take up too much of your time," said
Jake.

He briefly told her how he had found the note, and then related the strange events surrounding the theft of his clarinet. Mrs. Morton listened, and she nodded at Jake's suggestion that the thief may have been after the note rather than the clarinet itself. She took the note from Jake's hand and studied it. When she saw the handwriting, she squeezed her eyes shut as if to keep a painful memory away. "It's so strange seeing his handwriting again after all these years," she whispered, more to herself than to the teenagers. "Like looking in the bedroom mirror and seeing his reflection standing next to mine." She held the paper a moment longer, then passed it back to Jake. "It's Jerome's—Growler's—handwriting, all right. But I've never seen that note before. I don't know what it means."

"We were thinking," said Byte, "that it might help us understand what's going on if we knew a little more about your husband. What happened forty years ago?"

Mrs. Morton's face clouded with sadness. She let Byte's question hang in the air as she walked toward a couch and sank into one of its cushions. "Please," she said, "sit down." When Jake and Byte sat, the woman continued.

"That should be an easy question to answer, shouldn't it?" she said. "I mean, a husband and wife are in love, and the husband suddenly disappears. There should be a reason, right? An explanation that lets you say, 'this is a terrible thing, but I understand why it happened.'"

Jake pondered the woman's words, but it was Byte who first understood them. "Then you're not sure why he left," said Byte. "You're still wondering."

Helen Morton nodded. "I knew that Jerome— Growler—was in some trouble. He liked to look like a player, a high roller—always spending twice as much money as he had. He gambled a lot, borrowed money from the wrong kind of people. Worse, I believe he'd been doing it for a long time. He had reached a point, I think, where they had stopped caring about whether or not they got their money back. They were ready to make an example of him." A tear ran down her cheek, and she wiped a finger across it. "I just always assumed that he left because someone was after him, and he was afraid that I might get hurt if I was too close. That's what I tell myself. That he left out of love." Her eyes seemed to go vacant, as though she were slowly retreating from the room and the conversation. "I was singing that night. Growler was supposed to have been rehearsing with his band. I was so excited. We had been married less than a year, and I had just learned that we were going to have a baby."

"Scott," said Jake.

The woman smiled. "Yes. I couldn't wait to tell Growler. When I came home, and the apartment was empty—well, I can't describe the feeling. It was like my whole life, everything I wanted and hoped for, had been made of glass all along, and it was all cracking into little pieces."

"I don't want to upset you," Byte said carefully, "but the newspaper account of the disappearance mentioned some bonds that were stolen. The police wanted to question your husband."

Mrs. Morton turned her gaze on Byte. She looked as unapproachable as her son had when he first opened the door. "Young lady," she said evenly, "Growler Morton was not a thief." She rose then and gestured toward the hallway. The interview was over.

Helen Morton led Byte and Jake to the front door. They were just about to leave when Jake thought of another question. "Mrs. Morton," he said, "just one more thing. That night, when you came home—was there anything different in the apartment? Anything unusual—other than the fact that your husband was missing?"

Helen Morton paused, then began to shake her head no.

"Please," said Jake. "Is there anything you can think of that might help us?"

The woman thought a moment. "Well, all right, yes," she said slowly. "When I walked into the bedroom, I noticed that Growler had placed some of his belongings on the bed table. It was like he had arranged them, like he was creating a picture for me."

"What were the belongings?" asked Jake.

"The clarinet you bought. An old 45-rpm record, some sheets of music Growler had been working on, and a note to me."

"A note?" said Byte. "Do you mind if I ask you what it said?"

The lines across Helen Morton's forehead deepened. She appeared to struggle with the memory. Her voice dropped to a whisper. "All it said was, 'take care of my things.'"

"That's it?" Jake asked. "Just 'take care of my things'?"

"That was all. I never dreamed there was a message in the clarinet. I—I took the note literally and put his things away. I could hardly bear to handle them." She looked at Jake and Byte, seeming to *really* see them for the first time. She handed Jake's business card back to him.

"I don't care about the missing bonds," she said flatly, "or about stolen clarinets. My husband left me forty years ago, and I've never known if it was because he loved me too much—or not enough. If you could solve *that* mystery, I'd be forever grateful."

Scott Morton was standing at the door to usher them out. He shut the door behind them, feeling the heavy brass latch slip solidly into place. He twisted a handle so the door locked.

Then he moved around the house, locking *all* the doors.

He turned at the sound of his mother's footsteps. She was standing in the entryway to the den, her squared shoulders slumping now in weakness and exhaustion. She placed her hand on the wall to steady herself.

"Are you all right?" Scott asked.

She nodded. "I will be." She wrapped her arms around herself as though suddenly very cold. "Oh, God. It's going to happen again, isn't it?" she said. "The police will come after me, just like they did forty years ago. The stories will come out in the papers, and the authorities will start asking questions...."

She didn't finish the thought. Scott walked over to her and held her in his arms. Her head dropped to his shoulder, and she quietly began to sob.

"Don't worry," Scott said, "I'm not going to let that happen."

Peter Braddock swung his cherry red 1969 Volkswagen convertible into the parking lot of the RSA Records building. Mattie had recognized the building from the freeway—not that it was hard to spot. The massive brownstone, built in the 1930s, was a local landmark. A huge circle, designed to look like an old vinyl record, sat on the building's roof. In the center of the circle were the letters RSA, the S painted in jagged lines to resemble a lightning bolt.

Relaxing in the passenger seat, Mattie tossed a Lifesaver into the air as though he were flipping a coin. He caught the candy and covered it with his hand. "Heads or tails?" he asked, a mysterious grin on his face. Then he opened both hands, revealing that they were empty. An instant later Peter heard the candy crunching in Mattie's mouth.

"That one *is* impressive," said Peter, shutting off the Volkswagen's engine. The car rattled for several seconds before shutting down fully. "Okay, we're here. You remember the plan?"

"Sure," said Mattie. "My job is to basically shut up and let you do all the talking."

That stung. Peter looked at him. "Am I really that bad?" he asked.

Mattie grinned. "You can soothe my devastated ego by buying me French fries on the way home."

They made their way through a circular lobby filled with framed gold records, huge publicity posters, and autographed photos of longtime rock acts like Eric Clapton and Aerosmith, and jazz stars like Wynton Marsalis. A guitar, signed in bold red ink by each member of R.E.M., shone in a glass case.

"Wowwww," said Mattie.

Peter frowned as he looked about the room, wondering just how many of these names he should recognize.

A receptionist eyed them suspiciously through a shock of blue hair. "Help you?" she asked quickly.

As she spoke, an elderly woman wearing an ankle-length, lace-collared dress and a tan shawl passed by the desk. The receptionist called to her, waving a stack of files. Peter noted that she called the woman Agnes. Agnes eyed the two teens with an expression that reminded Peter of an illustration in a book he'd owned as a child. The book was *Hansel and Gretel,* and the illustration was of the witch, cackling over her crucible.

"Um, yes," replied Peter, turning his attention back to

the receptionist. "You can help us. Do you think some-one could spare a few minutes to talk to us about RSA and one of its artists?"

He had taken a chance by not calling ahead. Peter fig-ured it was harder to say no in person than over the phone, and he had a talent for talking his way into places. He had taken some jibes at school today for the tie he was wearing, but now, in the presence of this receptionist, it seemed to have the desired effect. She stared at it, mulling over the question, then reached for her intercom. "I doubt it, but we can try Mr. Bellows," she said, punching in an extension. "He'll talk to most anybody." Her tone took on a snide edge. Peter wasn't sure if she was ridiculing him or this Mr. Bellows. He finally decided it didn't matter, since he would get his questions answered either way.

After a brief, whispered conversation over the office intercom the receptionist said, "Awright. Second floor. Third office on the left."

Peter and Mattie found the office at the end of a long hallway. On the door, just beneath the word Sales, the name Derek Bellows appeared in gold lettering.

From the moment he entered the office, Peter's over-riding impression was that the record executive was a living, talking Ken doll. Bellows looked to be perhaps thirty years old. Coal black hair swept in a feathery pat-tern across his forehead, and the cleft in his chin reminded Peter of caricatures he had seen of Hollywood stars.

"Heyyyy," Derek Bellows said, pointing a finger, gun-like, at Peter. "Have a seat, guys. What can I do for you?" He tapped his fingers rhythmically along the top of his desk, as though a rock band were rehearsing in his head, and it was his turn to play drums.

"Thank you for seeing us," said Peter. He and Mattie perched a little uncomfortably in 1960s pop art chairs shaped like cupped human hands. "We're interested in the disappearance of Growler Morton," said Peter. "We thought that someone at RSA might be able to fill in some of the blanks."

"Aw*right*," said Bellows, "that's cool. A school assign-ment or something, right? I can help you there. Growler's kind of…well, you know, a mythic figure around here. Everyone in the building knows the story."

Peter threw a glance at Mattie. Growler's story was still so…*alive* here at RSA? And if so, was it because of the recent auction? Or was Growler a constant presence here at the company, like a ghost wandering the halls?

"What exactly happened forty-three years ago?" asked Peter.

"What happened?" repeated Bellows, shrugging. "We were ripped off, that's what happened. I mean, it hap-pened before my time, but the story goes something like this: Growler owed big money to some gangster types, okay? And he couldn't pay them back, right? So he disappears for a while. A week or so later he slips into our office after closing—I figure maybe he'd charmed the secretary enough times that he'd seen her turn the combination to the safe—and he swipes three mil. Then he's gone. *Bam!* No one ever sees him again."

Peter nodded, as though accepting Bellows' word, but he had long ago learned to assume nothing when questioning a source. Peter's father, a special agent for the FBI, said often that people's memories had the life span of soap bubbles.

"How do you know for sure that Growler stole the money?" Peter asked.

"It's the only answer that makes sense, man," Bellows said. "Like I told you."

Mattie cleared his throat. "Was the money ever found?"

Bellows shook his head. "Nah, man. It never was." Then he leaned forward and nodded at the two teenagers, his mouth forming a greedy leer. "The beauty of it is, man, is that it wasn't money the guy stole. It was bonds—negotiable, *interest-earning* bonds. If someone were to find them today, they'd be worth a fortune." He laughed.

Peter and Mattie stared blankly at him.

"Don't you get it?" he asked. "The insurance company reimbursed RSA at the time and later went out of business. So really, no one has a claim to the money! It belongs, all nice and legal, to whoever finds it. That'll make a good ending for your report, right?"

Peter looked again at Mattie. If Bellows were right, and the bonds were still out there somewhere, they would be worth many millions.

But the shared glance wasn't lost on Derek Bellows. His eyes darted back and forth between them. "So," he finally said, "what got you started on this, anyway? I mean, Growler Morton's not exactly a household name anymore. I figured two guys like you would be doing research on Britney Spears." He winked at them.

Peter smiled. "Let's just say we have reasons to be curious." He paused, unsure about how much information to share with Bellows, who went back to playing drums against his desktop. Peter sighed. "How long was Growler under contract here?"

Derek Bellows leaned back in his chair and tapped a pencil against his chin as he thought. "A little over a year," he said. He thought a moment longer, then tossed the pencil onto his desk, frowning. "Maybe. I think. Not very long, anyway." His shoulders heaved in a helpless shrug. "Actually, the person to ask would be my dad."

"Ask me what?" said a voice from the hallway. "Derek, did you forget our meeting?"

Peter turned and saw an elderly man entering the office. The man appeared to be in his early seventies, tall and trim, and he had cultivated the sort of deep, even tan that came only from a tanning booth.

"Oh, man! Yeah, I forgot. Sorry, Dad," Derek said, fumbling through the papers on his desk.

As the older man drew closer, Peter noted also that he had an odd scar on his left cheek. It was small, diamond-shaped, and it formed a dimple just above the man's jaw line.

"Guys," said Derek, "this is Franklin Bellows, my dad. He's the president here at RSA. If anyone can help you,

78 he can. He was a junior executive here back in the fifties. Actually, he's the man who signed Growler Morton to our label!"

The elder Bellows raised an eyebrow at the mention of the jazz musician's name. "Growler Morton?" he said. "Now there's some ancient history. Derek, I'm sure these young men would much rather hear about some of our more recent releases." He smiled at Peter and Jake. "Perhaps we can even find a promotional CD for them to take home, with our compliments."

"Thank you, sir," said Peter, "but we really are interested in Growler Morton."

"Yeah," said Mattie. "We were wondering if you could tell us a little about what happened with his disappearance and everything."

The younger Bellows looked up at his father, and the smile on his face suddenly seemed shallow and forced. "Yeah, Dad," he said, "fill us in about how ol' Growler stole those bonds." He laughed bitterly.

Just then the elderly woman Peter and Mattie had first seen in the lobby—Agnes, Peter recalled—entered the office across the hall and began filing the folders the receptionist had handed her. Peter studied the woman. She tugged at the file drawers angrily, stuffing the folders inside as though she hated the contents of each and every one. When she noticed Peter watching her, she smiled at him, revealing a set of large, yellow teeth. Peter looked away.

Peter then turned his attention to Franklin Bellows. Bellows said nothing, but Peter watched as the muscles in the record executive's jaw tightened. It didn't take a detective to realize that the president of RSA was trying to keep from losing his temper at his son's cavalier mention of the stolen bonds. "Listen," he finally said, "I take tremendous pride in this company and in the Bellows name, so you must understand that I find this subject upsetting. Growler Morton was the worst kind of thief. This company gave him his first chance as a recording artist. We—*I*—helped fashion his image. I suggest, for your own benefit, that you forget him. The man is dead. The bonds are gone. He betrayed us." Bellows glared at his son. "And you, Derek, should not be encouraging this kind of talk."

Peter was surprised at the man's barely controlled anger. He did not want to antagonize the elder Mr. Bellows any further, but the anger made Peter curious. "But if Growler Morton was never caught," said Peter, "and if the bonds were never found, what makes everybody so sure Growler was the one who stole them? Do you have any proof that he did it?"

The elder Bellows looked down at Peter, and his blue eyes narrowed. "A fair question," he said. "What have you read about Growler Morton? Did you know that he liked to impress people with his money? He wore a large ruby in a gold pinkie ring. It was his trademark." Bellows's voice softened, and he gestured toward a room down the hall. "A week after he disappeared, I discovered the bonds were missing and called the police. On the floor, in the carpet near the company vault, was the ruby. I recognized it instantly. Growler must have banged his hand

80 against something in the darkness and knocked the jewel from its setting."

Peter nodded. The ruby would certainly have been very strong circumstantial evidence that Growler Morton had committed the theft.

"Mr. Bellows," said Mattie, "have you ever heard the phrase 'One must look in the twenty-third place'?"

Peter poked Mattie with his finger, and Mattie let out a little yelp. Peter had not intended to reveal the Misfits' only clue—at least not before he'd tried every other plan he could think of—but now that Mattie had blurted it out, Peter could only hope they hadn't revealed too much.

Franklin Bellows thought a moment, then shook his head. "I'm not familiar with it, no," he said. "Where did you see it?"

Peter threw a sharp glance at Mattie, but Mattie had clamped his mouth shut and was massaging one rib.

"It's probably nothing," said Peter. "We found it in an old clarinet."

"Ah. I see," said the elder Bellows. "Well, my suggestion to you would be to ignore it. You're wasting your time. Growler Morton is dead, and the bonds will never be recovered." He rubbed his finger across the scar on his cheek, digging at it with a fingernail. "Now," said Bellows, smiling, "how about those promotional CDs, hmmm?"

Derek Bellows watched as his father escorted Peter and Mattie from the office. *Dear old Dad sure is pouring on the Bellows charm,* he thought. He stood at his window, gazing at the parking lot. A few moments later he watched as his two visitors drove off in an old Volkswagen Bug. *Freaky. The Morton stuff gets auctioned off, and two days later these guys show up asking questions.*

Derek Bellows had grown up around RSA Records, and he had heard whispers about Growler Morton ever since he was a child. Thoughts of the stolen bonds filled his mind every time he looked at the old photographs on his father's office wall.

As a teenager, he often stared at a particular photograph during those long periods when his father was ignoring him. The photo showed Growler Morton and his father shaking hands—his father's smile wide and plastic, the musician's smile weak and uncertain. Derek would look at that photograph, glare at the musician's image, and he would think of the missing bonds as belonging to him, the heir to the company. Franklin Bellows, whether or not he had time for his son, owned this company. The missing bonds should be a rightful part of Derek's inheritance.

And these teenagers seem to be hiding something, Derek reminded himself. The way the one kept glaring at the other, the way they never gave a straight answer...could they possibly have a clue to the bonds' whereabouts? And what was that odd phrase one of them mentioned?

82   Derek walked over to his desk and sat down. He grabbed a Post-it note from a pad and scribbled down the phrase before it escaped his memory. *One must look in the twenty-third place.* Derek didn't know what it meant, but nothing was going to stop him from finding out.

He heard a grinding. Derek spun around in his chair to see the old woman, Agnes, clearing the paper from the "shred" file. He then realized that the secretary, who had been with RSA since the early 1950s—and had known Growler Morton personally—had heard the entire conversation Derek and his father had had with those two high school kids. She was staring at Derek, and clearly *had* been staring for several moments. Was it possible that she?...

"Hey...hey, Agnes," Derek said. "'One must look in the twenty-third place.' Ever heard that?"

At first Agnes did not look at him. She continued feeding paper into the shredding machine, eyeing the spaghetti-like strips as they fell into the wastepaper basket. Then she focused her eyes on him for a few moments—just to let him know she had heard him call her—and went back to work.

Derek scowled at her. "Are you finished?" he demanded.

Without a word, the secretary strode past Derek, glaring at him with a look of utter contempt.

Early that evening Peter and Mattie arrived at Jake's house, quickly saying hello to Jake's mom in the den and waving to Jake's dad as they sped up the stairs. Jake and Byte were already there. Byte was typing away on her laptop. Jake sat against the side of his desk, lost in thought, bouncing a small rubber Superball so that it struck the floor, ricocheted off the wall, then arced upward and landed in his waiting palm. The rhythm of it was almost hypnotic.

"Okay," Jake said, his voice thick and stuffy through his swollen nose, "here's what we found out." He related the events that had taken place at the Morton home, emphasizing Helen Morton's insistence that Growler was innocent. Peter then filled them in on everything he and Mattie had learned about the theft of the bonds—including the fact that Growler's ruby was found next to the safe.

"I'm telling you, Peter," Jake said, "if you had seen the look on Helen Morton's face, if you had heard the way she talked, you'd *know* that Growler Morton did not steal those bonds." The ball bounced on the floor, ricocheted off the wall, then arced and landed in Jake's hand with a light *thwap*.

"That's what she *thinks*," Mattie said stubbornly. "You wouldn't want to believe someone you loved and trusted was a thief, would you?"

"He didn't do it," Jake insisted.

Peter frowned. "Hmmm. We certainly got a different story from RSA."

"That's for sure," said Mattie. "They're not big Growler Morton fans over there. And what about the ruby? They found it lying in the carpet right in front of the safe the bonds were taken from."

"Circumstantial evidence!" Jake said. "That doesn't mean—"

"You guys, shhh!" Byte said. "I need you to look at this." Mattie and Peter went to look over her shoulder at the columns of text on her screen. Above the columns was a reproduction of a black-and-white photograph. Byte adjusted the image so that the photograph dominated the screen's center.

"There's something else," said Byte. "While Jake and I waited for you guys to get back, I went into the newspaper morgue again to look at some of the other articles about Growler Morton. Look what I found."

Peter and Mattie leaned over so they could see the image more clearly. It was a photo of a bed table. On top of the table, arranged like a still life painting, were a clarinet, a 45-rpm record, and several sheets of paper.

"This was a follow-up article about Growler's disappearance," said Byte. "The photographer took a picture of the table just as Growler left it. That sheet of paper you see standing up is the note Growler left for his wife."

"'Take care of my things,'" said Jake.

"Right," said Byte. She pointed at the screen. "And here—you can barely see it because it's lying flat—is the sheet music to a composition Growler was working on just before he vanished."

Peter nodded. "I think I see where you're going with all this."

Byte tapped the screen. "Three items," she said. "Three things for Helen Morton to 'take care of.'" Byte turned toward Peter and Mattie, and the computer bathed half her face in an eerie, blue-gray light. "What if the note in Jake's clarinet was only part of the message? What if the other items are clues, or if there are clues inside them? Maybe we don't know what Growler was trying to say because we only have one-third of the message."

She sat on the floor and leaned her back against the wall. Sighing, she drew her knees up, wrapped her arms around them, and rested her chin against one bony kneecap. Peter's heart felt a light, jabbing pain as he watched her. He had seen her sit this way perhaps a thousand times. He had seen her grip the strap of her computer bag as though the bag were a life preserver. He had seen how, when she grew tired, her head would slip sideways against her shoulder and her eyelids would flutter. All these little gestures, these mannerisms, had suddenly turned into darts that struck him each time he looked at her, because he hadn't told her how he felt. She studied him with one eyebrow raised as though expecting him to say something.

Peter shook his head, rattling his mind back into focus. "Okay," he said, "so we have to figure out who has the other items. If they were auctioned, then we're lost. The auction house takes down the names and addresses of everyone who makes a purchase, but I'm sure the information is confidential. They'll never tell us who bought what."

Jake tossed his Superball again, and it slapped against his palm as he caught it. "We don't need the auction house," he said. "I remember who bought the record. It was the antique dealer, remember? His name was McCollum."

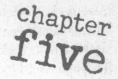

chapter five

Tuesday evening

Jim McCollum, the owner of McCollum's Antiques, stood on a stepladder to place a porcelain figurine on an upper knickknack shelf. He needed the ladder. McCollum was short and stocky. He had, however, the lean waist, thick chest, and heavily muscled arms of a bodybuilder. In his thick fingers, the tiny figurine almost vanished.

The tiny brass bell over his door jingled, and a tall, fair man with long, straw-colored hair and small, round, wire glasses entered the antique shop.

"Can I help you?" asked McCollum.

The man wandered over to a rolltop desk from the mid-1800s and brushed his fingers over the mahogany finish. "Beautiful," he said. "Today they make desks from pressed sawdust. Put a cheap veneer on top and pretend it's real wood."

McCollum nodded at the man as he moved about the store, browsing. He ran his finger across the edge of a crystal vase, listening to the hum of the rim. He tapped a nineteenth-century rocking chair so it swayed back and forth, its rockers ticking against the hardwood floor. He smiled and looked down his sharp nose at a seventy-five-year-old bicycle, chuckling as he rang its bell.

Finally the man approached the checkout counter.

His eyes were *incredibly* blue—almost violet, McCollum thought, like the sky just before twilight on a perfectly clear day. The man smiled at McCollum.

McCollum returned the smile and waited.

"I am looking," said the man, "for some old jazz music. I'm particularly interested in old 45-rpm recordings."

McCollum pointed to a display bin in a corner of the store. Dozens of old 45s stood within it, arranged in neat, alphabetized rows.

"Ah," said the man, still smiling. "Perhaps I need to have my glasses changed."

McCollum stared as the man walked over to the bin. *Too few customers in the store today,* he thought. On slow days, he sometimes had an irrational urge to follow a customer around the whole store, talking up every item and sounding like some pitiful sidewalk hustler.

The man walked over to the bin and began flipping through its contents. A few of the old records were jazz, and the man studied each, checking the labels for title and issue information. When he checked the last of them, he shook his head and returned to the counter.

"Most of your recordings are from the sixties," the man said. "I'm interested in older recordings by great soloists—Charlie Parker, Miles Davis, Thelonious Monk."

McCollum grinned. Like this customer, the antique dealer loved traditional jazz. "Oh, good luck finding any Bird," McCollum said. "Charlie Parker's old stuff in the original sleeve is worth a bundle."

"I know," said the man. "How about Stan Getz, then? Or Gerry Mulligan? Or Growler Morton?"

"Hey," said McCollum, "I'm a *huge* Growler Morton fan."

"Me too!" the man replied. He snapped his fingers, trying to remember something. "He had that amazing piece…now what was it? 'Rooster's Strut'?"

"Yeah," said McCollum, "the one with the *incredible* solo!"

"Yes, that's the one!" exclaimed the man. "Marvelous."

"I know, I *love* that piece," said McCollum, and the two men laughed.

The shopper leaned against the counter, his gaze once more circling the shop. "So," he said casually, "you don't have any Growler Morton for sale, do you? That would be quite a find."

"Nah," said McCollum, grinning. "But let me show you something. This'll blow you away."

He reached beneath the counter and took out the record he had purchased at the Morton auction. Smiling, he held it up so that his customer could read the label. "Check this out."

Upon seeing the title of the song, the customer gasped.

"You've got a copy of 'Whisper My Name'!" he said. "I can't believe it. Where on earth did you find this?"

"It's a first pressing," said McCollum, "in the original sleeve. And look at this…." He opened the paper wrapper to show the man the treasure he had found inside. "It's a note, signed by Growler Morton himself, see? I figure the autograph adds a least a hundred bucks to the value."

"Ahhhhh…." said the man. "I must have this! How much are you asking?"

McCollum turned and placed the record back on its shelf beneath the counter. "Sorry," he said, "it's not for sale. I bought it for my own collection."

The man nodded. "Too bad," he said, and then he offered a friendly grin. "Are you sure I can't change your mind?"

McCollum was momentarily tempted to listen to an offer, but the temptation was overridden by a sudden burst of determination. The antique dealer worked hard, and his shop supported him and his family, but it had not made him wealthy. He loved his business because it gave him the joy of finding treasures like this record. The wonder of finding Growler Morton's name scrawled on the inside of this pristine record sleeve was worth far more to him than any price this man would offer.

"Sorry," McCollum said. "No deal."

The man pulled his wallet from his jacket pocket. The wallet looked expensive to McCollum—and full. "Are you certain?"

McCollum shook his head. Though he could use the money, the record was more important to him. Case closed. "Sorry. I really am. I know you love the song, but I bought the record because *I* wanted it. It's not for sale. Now, if there's something else you want, or if you'd like me to call another antique shop for you, I'd be happy to oblige."

The man paused, the wallet wavering in his hand, and the smile faded from his face. He sighed, then put the wallet back into his pocket. "Very well, then," he said.

As he spoke, his eyes casually studied McCollum, focusing on the antique dealer's solid build and thick, muscular neck. As the man stared, McCollum felt a rush of adrenaline. The skin on the back of his neck prickled.

The man turned away from the counter, then spun his body around and delivered a powerful karate chop across McCollum face. McCollum sensed the blow coming, but his attacker was unbelievably fast. It happened so quickly—like those cheap martial arts films where the actors' movements are speeded up by the camera. The edge of the man's hand came down on the bridge of McCollum's nose, breaking it. McCollum's vision flared brightly as though a flashbulb had gone off, then a second blow struck his right temple. The antique dealer fell behind the counter, dizzy and clutching his head.

The man shot around the counter. McCollum struggled to his knees, and he caught a flash of what might have been regret in his attacker's eyes. Another blow landed just below his left ear, near the hinge of the lower jaw. McCollum saw another flash, and then everything went cold and black.

The man with long hair stood over McCollum's slumped body and drew in several quick breaths. He shook his hand and rubbed the sting from his fingers. Then he reached for the 45-rpm record, his whole body shaking.

He was angry with his client for not providing him with better information regarding this job, and he was angry with the antique dealer for making things so difficult. But most of all, he was angry with himself. His pride stung. Logan felt that a job, if properly planned and executed, should not require violence. Though he was well trained in the art of combat, it was an insult to his professional pride to have to use that training. Perhaps he could have found a more tempting argument to convince the antique dealer to sell the record; perhaps he could have flashed a wad of money so large McCollum could not have refused. Logan shook his head at the thought. McCollum, Logan sensed, was a proud man. Money would have just insulted him.

Perhaps he could have just come back later. But no, he'd had no choice but to act when the record was in front of him. If the antique dealer had taken the record home or stored it away because of its value, Logan would have needed two to three more days to scout and plan. He couldn't afford that much time. He'd had to take whatever steps were necessary to get the record now—tonight.

Complications. I hate complications! His last thought as he left the store—just as he was flicking off the lights and sliding the closed sign into place—was that he was beginning to wish he had never taken this crazy job.

Peter wouldn't mind sitting next to Mattie so much if he would just sit still for a minute. Mattie had been leaning forward in his seat, fidgeting the entire ride, and he kept spinning around to look out the back window when he missed a sign. Finally he pointed to a line of brick buildings that lay just ahead.

"There it is!" he shouted.

Peter did not acknowledge the shout. He was looking in the rearview mirror. Byte was sitting next to Jake—very close to Jake, actually. She stared absently out the window, her finger twirling a single lock of hair. Peter felt a little twinge in his chest. *What is she thinking,* Peter wondered, *staring out the window like that?* As his eyes flicked back and forth from the road to Byte's reflection in the mirror, Peter became suddenly aware of the pounding in his chest. What did that distant expression on Byte's face mean? Was there something sad, or wistful, in that quiet twirling of the hair? And did she have to be sitting that close to Jake?

"Hey, Peter," said Mattie, "you're going to miss the entrance."

"Oops—sorry," said Peter, whipping the car into the turn.

Bugle Point's downtown area was laid out in a large circle. When the mall and Wal-Mart arrived out by the freeway a few years earlier, the city council responded by spending millions to restore the downtown area. Now it had a quaint, period look.

"See those old-fashioned gas lamps?" asked Mattie. "They're wrought iron—supposed to look like they're from the early 1900s. The cool thing is that they've got digital timers and halogen bulbs. They look old, but they're state-of-the-art."

"I don't see what's so exciting about halogen bulbs," muttered Peter.

"What's bugging you?" asked Mattie.

Peter just glared at him. He remained stonily silent as he parked the Bug on a side street and the Misfits piled out. Byte slid out of the Volkswagen's rear seat. It seemed to Peter that she hesitated on the sidewalk just long enough for Jake to walk around the car and join her.

"It's at 121 Juniper Street," Mattie called as the group headed toward McCollum's shop. "Should be right around this corner."

They approached the building, but a plastic sign on the door indicated that the business had closed for the day. The lights were off, and through the lightly tinted window the store's insides looked like nothing more than a collection of monstrous shadows.

"We're too late," said Jake. "We'll have to come back tomorrow."

"But the sign says they don't close until seven," said Peter, looking at his watch. "It's only twenty of."

Byte frowned. "Hmmm. Well, the lights are off. Let's go home."

"Maybe he closed up because it was a slow day," Jake offered.

"Whatever. We'll have to come back tomorrow," Peter grumbled.

Mattie stepped closer to the door, cupped his hands around his eyes to cut out the glare, and pressed his face against the glass. The others started walking back to Peter's car.

"Mattie, we're out of here," called Jake, turning around and walking backward. "Come on."

"We're going to have to come back tomorrow," Byte shouted from down the sidewalk. Her foot caught a crack in the concrete, and she stumbled against Jake. Jake caught her to keep her from falling, and they both laughed.

"Sorry," she gasped.

"It's okay," Jake replied, smiling.

Peter watched them, his eyes narrowing, then forced himself to look away.

Mattie remained at the door of the antique store, silent.

"Mattie?" said Peter. "Come *on*."

Without a word, Mattie gripped the doorknob of the antique shop, turned it very slowly, and pushed. The door creaked open.

Peter stared at Mattie. The opening of the door seemed to open his mind again—to the case, to the Misfits' purpose for coming here. "Something's definitely wrong," he whispered to Jake and Byte. "Let's go."

"Great. Like I *wanted* to spend my evening prowling through a dark, closed antique shop," muttered Byte from behind him.

Peter strode up to Mattie. "All right," he whispered, peering into the dark shop, "how did you know that the door would be unlocked?"

Mattie pointed toward the checkout counter. An LED readout on the cash register glowed a bright green, showing the change that was due the last customer.

"Right," Peter admitted. "Even if McCollum closed up early and left the lights on, he wouldn't leave the cash register operating. Shopkeepers always turn off their registers, and sometimes they leave the empty drawer open. That way, a thief doesn't destroy an expensive cash register trying to get inside it." He shook his head. "I can't believe I didn't notice that."

"We better move slowly and quietly," warned Jake.

Peter gazed through the window one last time, then reached through the open door and flicked on the lights. The four of them entered the shop and spread out, stepping among the tables, chairs, and ancient highboy dressers crowding the space. Mattie, catching sight of a flash of silver, walked to the checkout counter to tap the button on a little chrome bell. He froze as he reached out to touch it.

A tiny groan escaped his lips. Peter saw Mattie clutch the counter as if to keep himself from collapsing.

"Guys!" Mattie called, his voice catching. "You better get over here. *Hurry!"*

They ran over and saw what Mattie was staring at. Behind the counter, lying twisted on the floor, was a man. A small trail of blood trickled from the man's nose and a dark bruise seemed to be forming across the left side of the man's head. One side of the man's jaw was red and swollen.

"It's McCollum," said Jake.

"He's breathing, at least," said Peter, noting the way the antique dealer's chest moved up and down. The injured man's eyes fluttered open, and he blinked several times before seeming to focus. McCollum looked up at the Misfits, his eyes flitting from one member of the group to another.

"Are you all right?" asked Peter.

McCollum blinked again and shifted his body slightly, as though measuring the extent of his injuries. Peter and Jake slowly lifted him to a seated position.

"Do you want us to call an ambulance?" asked Byte.

McCollum's eyes, the color of steel, locked in on the Misfits. "No," he said, mumbling around his sore jaw. "I'm…I'm all right. I can get myself to the emergency room."

"Did you see who attacked you?" asked Jake.

McCollum hauled himself to his feet, stumbling, but Jake caught his arm. He grabbed a tissue from a box on the counter and held it to his bloody nose. "Yeah," he said, "I got a good look at him. Big guy. Tall, muscular, in great shape. And *fast*. I've done some kickboxing, and I've never seen anyone that quick." He eyed the Misfits. "And you know what? This guy knew exactly where to hit me." He gently touched each of his injuries with his index finger, ticking them off. "The nose to incapacitate me, the temple to put me on the floor, the hinge of the jaw to knock me unconscious. The guy's a pro."

Peter grabbed a palm-sized spiral notebook from his pocket. "What did he look like?"

"Ummm…long blond hair," said McCollum, "hanging down to the middle of his back. Like a rock star." He paused. "Oh, yeah," he added, "and he had really unusual eyes. They were blue. I mean, *really* blue—blue like you've never seen."

Peter shrugged, scribbling down the detail.

"Did he get the Growler Morton record?" asked Jake.

McCollum suddenly looked beneath the counter, running his hand through scattered catalogs and loose credit card blanks. "The record!" he cried. "I stuck it right here after I showed it to the guy!"

"I guess that's a yes," Byte said.

McCollum stopped fumbling through his papers and gazed at each of the Misfits. "Hey," he said, "why are you asking all these questions? How did you know about the record?"

Peter handed McCollum one of the Misfits' business cards, patting him on the shoulder. "Maybe you better get your jaw checked at the hospital," he said. "Call us if you think of anything else." The Misfits filed out of the antique store and waited outside for McCollum to exit. Peter frowned, tapping his finger against the open pages of his notebook. "Two thieves," he said. "The old guy who stole Jake's clarinet, and now this long-haired martial arts expert." He looked at his friends. "That complicates matters."

"We have another problem," Jake said. "If our theory about the bonds is right—that the clues inside the objects are some kind of map to the bonds' location—then we have one of Growler's messages and the thieves have one."

Byte nodded her agreement. "And I think we can assume these guys have already got a line on the third one, too," she said in a glum voice.

They stood on the sidewalk for a few moments, silent. Jake, who had been slouching, drew up to his full height and took in a deep breath. "Well, come on," he said. "We're not just giving up, are we?"

McCollum stepped slowly from his shop. He moved a little unsteadily, flicking off the store's lights and fumbling for his keys. Once he had locked the door, he went to the corner and sat on a wrought iron bench.

100 "Maybe we won't have to," Peter said. "I've got an idea." He jogged over to where the antique dealer sat collecting his thoughts. "Mr. McCollum," he called, "do you need a ride to the emergency room?"

Mr. McCollum shook his head and gestured down a side road. "Nah, I'm fine, thanks," he said. "I just called my wife. She's coming to get me."

Upon seeing him up close, Peter thought that the bruise along the man's jaw had grown darker in just the last few minutes. He figured he better get what information he could quickly, then leave the poor man alone.

Peter chose his words carefully. "Sir, do you remember anything unusual about the record that was stolen? Anything at all?"

McCollum stared at Peter before responding. "Yeah," he finally said. "Yeah, I do. Growler Morton himself had written a little note in pencil. I found it on the inside of the sleeve." He sighed. "Man, what a collector's item."

"Do you remember what the note said?" Peter said eagerly. "The exact words?"

McCollum rubbed his eyes. "Yeah, yeah, yeah," he said. "Give me a second." He thought a moment, closing his eyes to visualize the note. "It said, 'Where lovers meet with open Arms.' The 'A' in 'arms' was capitalized. I have no idea what it meant."

"'Where lovers meet with open Arms,'" Peter repeated. "Are you sure that's exactly what it said?"

McCollum nodded, squeezing his eyes shut as though his head had begun to hurt again. "Yeah, kid," he said. "I'm sure, okay?"

"Thank you! Thank you for your help." Peter tried not to laugh out loud in delight. He ran back to the others. "We've got the second clue," he said, beaming. "We're in the game again."

Mattie gave Peter a high-five, and the Misfits made their way back to Peter's Volkswagen. Mattie, ecstatic, flipped a quarter high into the sky and snatched it from the air as it fell. Though Byte remained silent, the grin on her face grew ever wider as she approached the car. Only Jake lagged behind. He scuffed his shoe against the pavement. Mattie turned toward him, waving at him to hurry him up. "Hey, Jake," he called, "we're back on track. What's the problem?"

Jake stared at Mattie as though just realizing where he was. "Oh, nothing, I guess," he said finally. "I'm sure it's nothing to worry about."

The others remained silent, their eyes fixed on him.

"No, really," said Jake. "Forget it."

Mattie folded his arms, waiting. Byte raised her eyebrows at him. Peter just said, "Spill it."

Jake shrugged, surrendering. "Okay," he said, "okay." He took a deep breath and let it out slowly. "All right. It just seems to me that this old guy, the guy who stole my clarinet—well, at some point he's going to figure out that the clarinet doesn't have the clue in it, right? He's going to figure *I* have it, right?" Jake stared at his friends, a faintly pleading tone in his voice. "So doesn't that mean he has to come after me again?"

chapter
six

Later Tuesday evening

Karl Logan returned to his hotel, striding across the huge, crowded lobby and vanishing amid the tired business travelers and eager tourists. Once in his room, he flopped on the bed, grabbed the TV remote, and found a public television station airing a symphony concert. The screen's images played across his eyes, but he hardly saw them; instead, he stared vacantly, taking in the muted violins and cello and mulling over the events of the day.

He rarely felt anger while he was on a job. His work required precise planning and unfaltering concentration, and anger interfered with both.

But he was angry now.

The incident with the antique dealer had been unfortunate, but Logan had found that, in matters of small-time theft, the police were generally lazy. Really, the laziness was more a common-sense approach to fighting crime, a matter of finances. No law enforcement agency launched multi-million dollar investigations to recover clarinets and stolen records. Unless the victim of a petty theft could identify the thief, and the police knew where to find him, there was little chance the crime would ever be solved.

On the other hand, Logan knew, the local police's attitude changed remarkably when the robbery involved a physical attack. He knew their efforts to apprehend him would fail, but they might be a hindrance to his completing the job. Worse, if the police somehow managed to gather useful information about him or his methods, his future work might suffer as well.

Logan grimaced. All these problems because he had taken a job he did not like from a client he did not trust. Well, now he was committed, and he had to finish the job under the agreed terms. *Live and learn*, he thought. He knew he'd feel a lot better when he saw his fee appear in his Swiss account. Money wasn't everything, but it would help salve *this* wound.

Logan stalked to the bathroom, knowing the sooner he finished his work, the happier he would be. Removing the hairpiece, with its long, blond locks, was a delicate process, snapping open tiny clips and peeling up the porous fabric that formed the scalp. Once finished, he removed the small bits of latex he had used to change the shape of his nose and chin. Finally he looked down at the floor and blinked his eyes; with a practiced hand, he popped out the contact lenses that changed his eye color from brown to blue.

It was time to report.

He removed the cell phone from his briefcase and dialed the number for his client. He waited three rings, and a voice answered.

"Yes?"

"It's me," said Logan. "I have the second item."

No reply came, and Logan thought he heard a door shutting in the background. Apparently, his client wanted privacy.

"Do you have it in front of you?" Logan heard an edginess in the voice that made him uneasy. Edgy clients were unpredictable.

"It's right here," said Logan. He reached for the 45, preparing to describe it if necessary.

"Tell me," said the client. "Is there anything unusual about it?"

Logan saw nothing at first glance, but then he remembered the writing the antique dealer had showed him. It was in pencil, and a little difficult to read against the yellowing paper, but the words were clear enough.

"Yes," said Logan. "There's a note on the inside of the sleeve. It says 'Where lovers meet with open Arms.'"

Logan waited through several moments of silence, wishing that he and his client were face to face. He would have a better sense of what was going on if he could see the other person's gestures and expressions.

After another pause, the client spoke again. "I see. Then I was right to be concerned. We have another problem."

Great, thought Logan. *Just what I need.*

"You should have found a similar note in the clarinet too. I've been over the instrument several times since you brought it to me, and I've found nothing."

Logan wasn't impressed. "I see," he said. "Then I guess *you* do have a problem."

"*I'm paying you a fortune to handle my problems!*" snapped his client. Logan heard ragged, uneven breathing as the client's desperation grew. "There must have been a note. I'm certain of it. You said you stole the instrument from a teenager. He must have the note. Get it from him."

Logan almost laughed. "Do you have any idea how difficult it would be, and how risky, to plan a second theft? Forget it. I did what you hired me to do. I faced some...complications today, and things have gotten a little hotter than I'd like."

"But—but—you *have* to get the note!" the muffled voice practically shouted. "The clarinet means nothing to me. It's the *note* I need."

Logan felt his lips tighten into a thin line as he fought to control his own anger. "Well," he said, "maybe that's been our problem all along. We're not really communicating, are we? You wanted a slip of paper, but you asked me to steal a clarinet. From the beginning, I've been operating with only half the information I need to do my job effectively. I think it's time I got the whole story."

The voice on the other line hesitated. "Well...well, all right, then. But you have to promise me you'll get the note. Now that you've described the record to me, my worst fear is confirmed. I *have* to have the other items."

Logan kicked his shoes off and sprawled on his back across the bed. He propped his head up with a couple of pillows. "All right," he said. "Make this good, and I'll see about dealing with the teenager."

The Misfits returned to Jake's house. Byte sat on the floor and tapped on her keyboard, searching through various permutations and meanings of the number twenty-three. Sadly, the best she had come up with was a quote from the twenty-third Psalm, a list of the top twenty-three sidewalk cafés in Boston, Massachusetts, and information about the twenty-third amendment. She scrolled through lists. "A baseball is twenty-three centimeters in circumference," she said in a tired voice. "Shakespeare was born on April 23 and died on April 23…Lou Gehrig hit twenty-three grand slam home runs… 'W' is the twenty-third letter of the alphabet.…"

"Enough," groaned Mattie. "If I confess, will you stop?"

Jake took a clarinet reed from its box and began sucking on it as he stared out his bedroom window. Peter eyes followed him. Jake touched a finger against the side of his nose and winced. The deep, blue-black bruise that ran along his cheekbones and across the bridge of his nose was taking on hints of green here and there. He glanced at Mattie and made a honking sigh. Peter understood.

On the way in, Mattie had swiped a fistful of Oreos from the kitchen cabinet and was now sitting on Jake's bed, stuffing the cookies into his mouth one after another.

Frowning, Peter went back to work. He held Growler Morton's note in his hand and smoothed out its curled, yellowed edges so he could read it. The ancient paper unrolled with a dry crackle.

One must look in the twenty-third place.

He stood and walked over to Jake's desk. There he found a pad and pen and wrote out the second clue, the one the Misfits heard from the antique dealer.

Where lovers meet with open Arms.

He stared at the words, but nothing came to him. He looked at Byte sitting next to Jake, and she seemed to shift a little. *Is she uncomfortable, or did she shift to be closer?* Peter fought the urge to crumple the note in his fist. *Concentrate!* he told himself. He knew that understanding these messages was the key to solving this mystery, but right now figuring them out seemed as difficult as trying to assemble a jigsaw puzzle without ever having seen the picture on the top of the box. *Stop letting things distract you,* he scolded himself.

Human DNA has twenty-three chromosomes....

He sighed. "Okay." He let the slips of paper drop from his fingers and flutter to Jake's desktop. "I'm stumped."

Mattie's eyes widened in feigned surprise. "And you admit it?"

Jake and Byte laughed, and even Peter grinned weakly at the comment.

Byte sighed. "Nothing else here," she admitted, shutting down her computer.

"Let's go over what we have," said Jake.

"We know that Growler Morton disappeared more than forty years ago," said Peter, "that he was never seen again, and that he left at least two messages behind—one rolled up inside an old clarinet, the other scribbled on the inside sleeve of a 45-rpm record."

"We also know," said Byte, "that he was in some kind of financial trouble when he disappeared. Both Mrs. Morton and the guy at the record label confirmed that."

Mattie nodded. "And we know that, just a few days after Growler vanished, three mil in bonds were stolen from his record label. On top of that, Mr. Bellows told us that a jewel from his ring was found right next to the company safe the morning after the robbery." Mattie shrugged as though the solution to the case were elementary. "Nothing against you, Peter," he said, "but it's not like we have to call in the detectives from *NYPD Blue* or something. Growler had some trouble, stole the bonds, and he's either dead or having a great time on his yacht somewhere."

Jake frowned. "Hey," he said, "do we know if the bonds were even cashed?"

"After forty years," said Byte, "how would we find out? I've been all over the Net, and I can't find anything."

Peter rubbed his eyes. "Something about this whole thing…I don't know, it just doesn't feel right. We just can't automatically assume that Growler stole the bonds.

09

I know the situation looks bad for him, but all we have is circumstantial evidence."

Byte nodded. "Right. Growler stole the bonds, and *then* what? Why did he never contact his wife? Why did he—or his body—never turn up? How did his wife get such an expensive house? And what do the written clues mean?"

A lock of hair fell across Peter's eyes. He started to calmly brush it aside, but a sudden fit of frustration caused him to close his hand into a fist, grabbing the hair and tugging at it.

"You'll go bald if you keep doing that," said Byte. She grinned at him, and Peter, eyeing his hand, let go of the hair and began to pace.

Mattie hauled himself onto Jake's desktop. "What about the thieves?" he asked. "What do we know about them?"

"Hmm? Oh." Peter glanced at his spiral notebook, flipping the pages to McCollum's description of the attacker in the store. "Okay, the guy who stole the record was relatively young, had long blond hair, and apparently knew a lot about martial arts."

"Great," said Mattie. "Why is it that so many bad guys know how to fight? I mean, aren't there any thieves out there who look like *me*?"

Byte and Jake burst out laughing.

Peter just smiled. He tapped his notebook. "McCollum also mentioned something about the guy having unnaturally blue eyes." He flipped to the next page. "His exact words were 'blue like you've never seen.'"

110   "Oh, well, *that* certainly narrows things down," said Mattie.

Jake turned to face Peter, nodding to himself as though remembering something. "Wait a minute," he said slowly. "That's *right*. The old guy who jumped me also had weird eyes. They were a really intense green. I've never seen eyes that color before."

"A family trait?" suggested Mattie. "Like maybe we've got a father/son team?"

Peter snapped his fingers. "Or *contact lenses*," he cried. "The colors of tinted contacts are really intense, almost unnatural. They'd be a great disguise for someone who wanted to hide his eye color." He looked at Jake, thinking. "And it explains a lot—like how an old man could beat up a two-hundred-pound teenager."

"What are you saying?" asked Mattie.

Peter shook his head. "Guys," he said, "I think we have to consider the possibility that we're dealing with only one thief. We better call Decker and tell him."

He folded the sheet of paper and tapped it against his open palm. Jake took his tiny Superball from his pocket and bounced it against the floor. Byte, silent, removed her glasses and rubbed at the red pressure marks they left on her nose. The room remained silent for a very long time.

Finally Mattie looked up, eyeing each of them. "Listen," he said quietly, "there's one other thing we haven't talked about." He paused, fidgeting as though

uncomfortable with his own thoughts. "What if Growler **111**
Morton himself is behind this? What if he's still alive?"

Helen Morton sat on her living room floor, taping
down the lid of another cardboard box. She was almost
finished—at least for tonight.

Her eyes rose to the mantel, where she had once placed
all her knickknacks—the Royal Doulton figurines, the
crystal angels, the bronze bust of Growler a friend had
cast long ago. Now all these pieces lay in Bubble Wrap,
surrounded by Styrofoam and cardboard. Only one
item remained on the shelf: a music box. Helen picked it
up and rubbed her finger against its smooth, porcelain
finish.

She couldn't explain why she hadn't packed the music
box with everything else. It wasn't that she had forgotten. Her memory for detail had always been exceptional.
Even these days, she didn't bother with personal phone
directories or shopping lists. What she needed to
remember, she remembered.

By this point, most of her clothing was boxed; so were
the china and silver—and almost everything in the
kitchen.

And yet, here was the music box. It had been a
Christmas present from Growler, oh, so many years ago.
He had tried to find one of a couple waltzing together,
but could only find this one—a woman dancing alone.

She held it in her hand, hesitating to put it away. She touched its mahogany base and studied the brass key that turned the winding mechanism. She gripped the key and began to turn it. The music box whirred, and the figure on top—a tiny dancing girl with a porcelain white face, pink lips, and cherry drop cheeks—began to dance. She wore a pink taffeta dress and white leggings. Her shoes were black and so very tiny, painted with a surgeon's steadiness. The music, Helen remembered, was something from Strauss.

She watched it like an old woman staring at a photograph of herself as a beautiful young girl. The little porcelain figure danced, spinning to the whir of a tiny motor.

Helen watched the figure silently, then touched a switch near the base of the box. The music stopped suddenly, and a harsh silence filled the room.

A door opened behind her. She glanced over her shoulder and smiled as Scott entered. He wore a pair of jeans he had long ago ruined with paint and a sweatshirt that was torn at the shoulder and streaked with grime.

"How's the packing?" he asked, making his way through the maze of boxes to where she stood.

"Still quite a bit left to do," she answered, hugging him. "I see you've finished clearing out the garage."

He laughed and looked down at himself.

Helen Morton wrapped the little dancer in tissue paper, bent down, and placed it in a cardboard box. She closed the lid and sealed it shut with tape.

"I'm surprised you didn't auction that off," Scott said.

"I kept some things," she said quietly.

He put an arm around her shoulder, then guided her to the couch and sat her down. "How are you feeling?" he asked.

"Feeling?"

"About the move," he said. "About selling the old furniture and Dad's things."

She smiled. "Life will be simpler," she said. "This big house is filled with memories. Moving into a smaller space, new surroundings. Letting go of the past. The change will be good for me."

"And it's closer to my family," he reminded her. "I'm glad about that."

She smiled.

Scott squeezed her hand. "No regrets, then?"

"None," she said. "And how about you?" She studied her son carefully. Scott, at forty-two, looked like a much younger man. He had no laugh lines around his eyes to add age to his face. Helen realized suddenly with tremendous sadness that she had not seen her son laugh very often. Instead of laugh lines, his age showed more subtly in the two deep wrinkles in his forehead—anger lines from frowning.

Scott had grown up so angry. She often wondered if it might have been better if she had not told him so much about Jerome, had not filled his mind with romantic images of a father he never would know. He'd always had so many questions, always scouring through the old photographs. Perhaps, too, she had told him too much of what had happened later—with the police, the accusations.

She studied him now. "I worry about *you* letting go of the past," she said.

Scott remained silent. He gave her a kiss on the cheek and rose from the couch.

"We'll expect you for dinner on Sunday," he reminded her.

When he was gone, Helen walked over to an antique cedar chest that lay against the wall. She opened the chest and looked at the items she had stored inside— some linens, her wedding album, her husband's finest clarinet, a scrapbook.

Helen reached for the memory album and opened it. Inside were pages of photos, some going back as far as her honeymoon. Some pages contained news clippings about Growler. She even found a photo of herself— young, her body shimmering in a silver lamé gown, singing into a microphone in front of Growler's band.

In the back of the album were some sheets of musician's staff paper. Over time, they had yellowed, and a few years ago Helen had taken them to a specialist who repaired old books. He brushed a solution onto the paper that, he said, would prevent it from deteriorating further. Now, as Helen held the sheets in her hand, she was happy she had gone to the trouble. The pencil markings on them were in Growler's own hand.

It was the last song he had ever composed. Helen smiled now as she looked at the crude slash marks that served as notes. Growler never had the patience to bubble in the notes the way they might appear on a piece of printed music.

She looked at the top of the page, at the title of the piece: "Waltz with Helen."

Growler had finished it on the day he disappeared. Helen, who could sing but could not read music, had never heard it played. The months after Growler vanished had been so hectic, so terrifying, she had never thought to take the sheet music to another musician. Later, when she had come to accept her husband's disappearance, she had decided the piece was better left unplayed. She had built up in her mind an image of the song, had heard it a thousand times in her dreams, and she knew that the reality might not live up to the fantasy. Another musician could read the notes, but would play without the benefit of Growler's ear or Growler's heart. She feared the song would seem sterile and empty.

Helen Morton smiled, closed her eyes, and pressed the loose sheets against her body. It was time to let go of the house—time, even, to let go of the past. But she would hold on to some things.

This song was Growler Morton's last gift to her. She returned it to the cedar chest, and the sweet smell of the wood lingered in the air after she closed the lid.

seven

Wednesday morning

derek Bellows sat behind the wheel of his Corvette, his foot nudging the accelerator, easing the speedometer past sixty. The stereo system—a two-hundred-watt Kenwood monster—pounded as he drove. Punk music by Black Flag blared from his windows. The music—not Derek's favorite—pulsed with an anger that was almost blinding. A person could lose himself in that anger. Derek jabbed his finger at the volume control until the bass and drums throbbed. He felt them in his bones.

He made a right turn and found a parking place across the street from Bugle Point High School. Eyeing the school entrance, he shut off the engine and waited, his heart pounding and his breathing ragged.

The dashboard clock showed that it was ten minutes past seven, and the first students were beginning to arrive on campus. Derek had scouted out the school the previous afternoon, and he was pleased to note that cars entered through only one driveway and exited through another. Every car entering the school would have to pass directly by him.

Perspiration beaded on his forehead even though the morning was cool. The windshield of the Corvette began to fog, and he hurriedly wiped it with his shirt-sleeve.

Around seven-thirty, the traffic thickened. Cars streamed through the gate, and Derek watched each one closely. Many of the cars were boxy hatchbacks, compact models of one indistinct make or another. Others were run-down muscle cars—Trans-Ams or Firebirds, fifteen to twenty years old and rattling badly, but dream cars for seventeen year olds working for minimum wage. Scattered among these were a few sport utility vehicles and an occasional Mercedes or BMW.

But Derek was looking for something more unusual.

At seven-forty a cherry red 1969 Volkswagen Beetle convertible approached the school and turned right, into the driveway. Derek watched as the tiny car circled the parking lot. It came to a stop, and a teenager stepped out. Derek smiled. The kid was skinny, and he wore owlish glasses with big, round frames. A clump of black hair fell across his forehead and into his eyes. It was the same kid who had come into his office, the kid who knew something about Growler and the money.

Derek waited a while longer. At seven fifty-five a bell rang, signaling the start of first period. The parking lot was empty. Except for a few stragglers, the students had gone to class. Derek stepped from the car. He walked onto the campus, eyeing the area for a security officer, and headed toward the VW. His heart was still pounding—now, oddly enough, to the chaotic rhythm of a stupid Black Flag song.

Derek swallowed hard. He would have to work quickly.

When he reached the VW, he crouched down so that the cars around him formed a cover. From his jacket he pulled a thin strip of metal a little over an inch wide and about two feet long, with a notch cut in one end. Derek slid the Slim Jim between the Volkswagen's driver side window and the rubber molding in the door, where—after several moments of Derek's nervous fumbling—the notch caught on a steel rod. Then Derek gripped the end of the tool and pulled. The lock popped open.

It's amazing what you can learn, he thought, *when you bribe a crooked locksmith.*

Derek then slid inside the VW and reached into his pocket for a small circular microphone an inch and a half in diameter and no more than half an inch thick. On the back of the microphone was a small but powerful magnet. Derek's palms were sweating. He fumbled with the device, then steadied it and closed his eyes, forcing himself to calm down.

I know I can do this, he told himself.

Derek had bought the bug through an advertisement in the back of *Soldier of Fortune* magazine, which he had purchased, red-faced, from a tattooed man who operated a dingy gun shop outside of town. The used bug was an obsolete model, but had still set him back two hundred bucks, plus the extra twenty for overnight shipment. Derek had studied the owner's manual at home, wanting to be prepared for this moment. But now, when he needed to think, he found he couldn't breathe normally, his hands wouldn't stop shaking, and he couldn't remember the instructions. Frustrated, he pulled the manual out of his pocket and riffled through the pages until he found the diagram he needed.

There....

Bending down so he could see beneath the dashboard, he located a section of exposed metal. The magnet on the back of the bug snapped against it and held the metal firmly. Next he found a tiny switch on the side of the microphone and flipped it to the right. A red indicator light clicked on, confirming that the microphone was now pulling juice from its tiny battery. It was working, and would keep working for about a week.

They'll never know, Derek told himself. He held on to the thought the way a child in a large crowd might hold on to his mother's hand. *They'll never know. They'll never know.*

Derek let out a deep breath and sat up in the seat. He looked around, making sure no one was looking in his direction, then stepped from the car.

He shivered slightly as he walked away.

The bug had a mile radius. When the kid and his friends got in that car, Derek would be able to hear every word they said, as long as he stayed reasonably close to them. Derek decided to slip from the office and hang out by the school each morning as classes started and again in the afternoon when classes let out.

Walking stiffly back to his car, he realized his leg muscles had cramped from tension and from crouching under the VW's dash. Behind him, footsteps scuffed the concrete, their pace steadily increasing as though someone were walking, then walking faster, then running. Derek increased his pace as well. He didn't want to run—too suspicious—but sweat poured down his cheeks and onto his collar as he strode quietly toward the Corvette. He imagined a hand coming down on his shoulder, a voice calling his name, and the thought made his knees go weak.

"Hey, you!" someone shouted. Derek froze. He turned around very slowly—to the sight of a skinny kid wearing jeans and a Seattle Seahawks football jersey. The kid pointed at Derek's left foot. "Dude," he called, "your shoelace is untied."

The tightness in Derek's throat kept him from speaking. He nodded, bent down on one knee, and tied his shoelace.

The teenager ran past him, nodding a quick goodbye. Derek smiled, formed his fingers into the shape of a gun, and said, "Heyyyy, thanks."

Karl Logan sat in his hotel room and pondered his current problem. Last night his client had explained everything. More precisely, his client had cracked like an ancient piece of pottery, spilling out the truth. Before the conversation ended, the two parties had come to a new agreement, one that provided Karl with even more money than his original contract called for. The rules were simple. Growler Morton had left three items—and three messages—for his wife. Karl's job was finished when he delivered all three.

He pulled a stack of photographs from his briefcase. These images were his initial research, the observations he had made from a distance during the Morton auction. He flipped through them, matching the item in each photo to the auction program and to the notes he had taken. Karl remembered each item quite vividly, but he insisted on being thorough in his work. When he finished, he flipped through the photographs a second time.

He found nothing, no mention at all of a sheet music manuscript. Karl was not surprised, since he didn't remember such an item in the auction, but the result was still disappointing. In the odd event that he had missed something, he pulled out his laptop and once again hacked into the system at Starlight Auctions. Their records, as well, showed no mention of a piece of original sheet music.

To relax his mind and allow it to work on the problem, Karl sat on the floor of the hotel room and crossed his legs beneath him. Then he closed his eyes and laid his hands, palm up, on his kneecaps, assuming the lotus position. Karl found that yoga kept him limber, and being flexible was an important adjunct to his martial arts training. More importantly, yoga quieted Karl's thoughts; it settled the turbulence that churned inside him when a job brought on extra pressures.

Karl breathed slowly and emptied his mind. In a few moments, when he was completely relaxed, an answer would come.

Meditation sometimes played havoc with his sense of the passage of time. When giving himself fully to the process, Karl could not say if he remained in the lotus for five minutes or half an hour. During this time his thoughts calmed and organized themselves. His mind cleared. Once he completed the meditation, he could look at his problem coldly, logically, and assume with confidence that his efforts would find a solution.

Minutes later, he opened his eyes, drew in several deep breaths, and analyzed his problem.

Observation: No piece of sheet music was offered for sale at the Morton auction. That much was fact, so Karl looked, one by one, at the possible explanations.

One: The Morton woman could still be in possession of the music. Here, Karl thought, was a likely possibility. The sheet music was reported to be in the musician's own hand, which would make it a particularly personal item to Helen Morton.

According to the news reports, the note on the bed table said "Take care of my things." Mrs. Morton could very likely have taken this instruction to heart. In forty years, she might lose interest in an old clarinet neither she nor her son could play, or in an old recording of a song that was readily available—and sounded better—on CD. But a piece of sheet music, something her lost husband had written just for her, *that* she might not give up. The more Karl pondered the idea, the more certain he became.

Still, to be thorough, he would consider other options....

Two: In the forty years since Growler's disappearance, the sheet music could have been lost or destroyed. In this case, Karl could proceed no further. Fortunately, since his client seemed less interested in acquiring the music than in preventing someone *else* from acquiring it, the loss of the music was not a problem. If he could prove that it no longer existed, Karl's job was finished.

Three: The music had been stolen and was now in someone else's possession. This was the nightmare scenario. The only plan in that case would be to identify the thief, who may have had decades to cover up his tracks, and locate the music. It would be nearly impossible to do so. His client would have to live with this fact, and Karl would have to accept a lesser payment for a half-finished job. Karl found no satisfaction in this option.

No, Karl thought, his first impulse had to be correct. To acquire the sheet music, he would have to start with Helen Morton.

Byte hunkered over her laptop and opened the file for her trigonometry glass. She was glad that Mrs. Dworkin had come to be so open-minded about letting her use her computer. Some teachers distrusted anything more modern than a #2 Ticonderoga.

Some students were even more out of touch than teachers. As she typed, Byte felt eyes boring into her. She glanced up to see Rachel Hingis, the Student Council secretary, staring at the laptop. Rachel then glared at Byte, and her hands moved as though she were typing into a keyboard. "Tack-tack-tack-tack-tack," she muttered, her tongue ticking the sounds off angrily. "Drives me *crazy*."

Byte leaned over and glanced at Rachel's paper. "Your cosine's off," she said.

"Wha—?" Rachel's eyes shot down to her trig work, scanning each line of figures. "Where'd I go wrong? I don't see it," she said to herself. "I don't see it," she repeated, like an accident victim in shock. "I don't see it...."

After the nasty crack, Byte was tempted to let Rachel suffer through trig on her own, but she knew she'd feel a pang of guilt if she didn't help. Byte looked at Mrs. Dworkin to make sure the teacher was occupied, then angled the computer so Rachel could see the screen. Byte's laptop contained a trig program that was about a hundred times faster and more complex than the tiny, expensive graphing calculators other students carried. While Rachel's calculator drew a curved line—

point by agonizingly slow point—across its two-inch display, Byte's laptop flashed her work in full color on a fourteen-inch screen. A thin red line snaked one from end of the display to the other—a perfectly constructed sine wave. Beneath it were the figures Byte had input, and overlaying the entire image was a fine cross-hatching of graph lines.

"That's so awesome," Rachel whispered. She gazed at Byte's figures, then at her own. Her sine wave carved its path across her screen, its peaks turning jagged then dipping as though they were mapping out the face of a cliff.

Rachel cleared her work and started over. "Hmph," she said, a hint of snideness lingering in her tone. "Guess I should say thanks."

Byte barely heard Rachel. She found herself staring at the computer screen, at the figures lining the bottom of the image, at the beautiful sine wave arcing up and down. Her work was perfect. Though she used a computer every day, she never lost interest in them and the amazing things they could do. To Byte, it seemed computers could solve any problem—well, except for how to get a certain clarinet player to pay a little more attention to her. *Almost* any problem, then. A computer could start with a million possibilities and bring you down to one—the answer.

That's it! Byte felt a tingling between her shoulder blades, which slowly crept down her back and along her arms.

She grabbed a pencil and some paper from her folder—sometimes carrying the stuff *was* necessary—and began scribbling three quick notes, telling the other Misfits to meet her in the library at lunch. Then she folded the notes and drew the circle/square emblem on the outside of each one.

She would run into Mattie during the morning break. He would get the notes to the others.

When the lunch bell rang, Byte practically ran to the library. When she arrived, she saw that Peter was already waiting for her. A moment later Jake and Mattie sauntered in.

Byte led them behind the checkout counter and over to the librarian's desk. Ms. Langley was scanning new books into the library's system—a pen clenched, as always, between her teeth—and she raised an eyebrow at the crowd of students invading her personal territory. Byte held up her computer bag for the librarian to see, but Ms. Langley just plucked the pen from her mouth and folded her arms in mock surprise at Byte's boldness. "Oh," she said. "Just because you were my aide last semester you think you can waltz in here any time and tie up my phone with that..." she pointed at the computer, "*machine?*"

Byte smiled. The library had computers, of course—and at least half a dozen of them were Internet-connected—but Byte preferred her own laptop with its gutsier processor and speedier modem. "Pleeeeaase?" she asked, playfully drawing out the word.

Ms. Langley shook her head and surrendered. "All right," said the librarian. "Just promise me you're not ordering a pizza. I'm trying to watch my weight, and I can't say no to Domino's."

Mattie waved. "Hi, Ms. Langley."

"And *you*, Mr. Ramiro, can take that little multi-tool from your pocket and set it right on my desk where I can keep an eye on it. You can pick it up on your way out."

Jake nudged Mattie's shoulder. "I told you so," he whispered. "You shouldn't have taken apart her cell phone last year."

"I *did* get it to work again…eventually," mumbled Mattie.

Peter put a hand on Mattie's shoulder, guiding him toward a table. "Let's be quiet and stay out of her way," he said as Byte began to set up her computer. "If she finds out what we're up to, she might shut us down."

Byte struggled to connect the phone cord to her modem jack. "I was using my computer in first period, and it suddenly occurred to me that we might be able to use a database type of search engine to figure out what happened to Growler Morton." She booted up her system and dialed the number for the newspaper morgue.

"How?" Mattie asked.

"Well," she said, "More than forty years have passed since Growler Morton disappeared. What's the likelihood that he's still alive?"

"Well, if he were alive, he'd be in his seventies," said Mattie.

"That's not too old. Maybe he's alive, and he's come out of hiding because he somehow feels threatened by the potential discovery of the clues," Jake offered. "But why wouldn't he have gotten in touch with his wife during all of these years to let her know he's all right?"

"We don't know for sure that she only knows as much as she says she does," Peter pointed out. "She says he's never contacted her, but she could have a reason to lie."

"Well, if he's alive, this won't help much. But he *may* be dead and buried," Byte said, typing away.

Mattie frowned at her.

"I'm just trying to think like a detective!" Byte went on. "It's a pessimistic way to approach the problem, but by the process of elimination, we might be able to figure out what happened to Growler."

"Right," agreed Peter. "We have to consider the fact that Growler wouldn't have been living under normal conditions. If he's survived, he's survived underground. Some pretty disreputable people were after him when he disappeared—not to mention the police. He would be living on the run."

Byte was keying in the search instructions for the newspaper's database. "Well, if he's dead, his death was bound to have been reported at some time—even if the body wasn't identified."

Mattie peered over her shoulder and frowned. "You're asking the morgue to list *every* death that the paper has reported in the last *forty years?*"

"The digital files wouldn't go back that far," Byte said. "But the newspaper has been scanning in the actual pages little by little. Maybe we'll find something."

"This is a long shot," Mattie muttered.

Byte stuck her tongue out at him and hit the return key. The instruction ran at 56,000 bytes per second to the database in the newspaper's mainframe. A moment later, a figure appeared on Byte's screen.

```
Number of matches found................148,279
```

"Boy, that makes our job easier," Jake said.

"Don't be sarcastic," said Byte. "We're not done yet. Now we start screening with narrower parameters."

Peter nodded. "I get it. Okay, Growler was a man. Let's start with that."

"Right," said Byte. She added the words **Gender: Male** to the search instructions, and the computer ran its search again. After several moments, it responded.

```
Number of matches found................82,497
```

"He was African-American," added Mattie.

Byte nodded silently as she typed in the instruction. "I'm not sure what the accepted term was when Growler died, so I better cover them all." She ordered the computer to seek out articles referring to a male who was black, Negro, Afro-American, or African-American.

```
Number of matches found................24,927
```

"Still way too many to be useful," said Peter. He thought a moment, then tapped the screen thoughtfully. "Wait," he said. "Growler's body wasn't identified, so the police would have used a generic name when reporting his death."

"John Doe?" replied Jake.

Byte nodded and typed in the name authorities gave to a male body they could not identify.

Name: Doe, John.

Mattie grabbed one of the wooden chairs and turned it around, straddling it. "Would a newspaper do an obituary on a John Doe?" he asked.

"No," said Peter, "but we're not looking for an obituary. If Growler is dead, he may well have died violently—which would have been reported as a murder or an accident. So we're looking for a news brief."

The computer whirred, then stopped. This time, the search was noticeably shorter than before.

Number of matches found...............215

"Excellent!" said Jake.

"Yeah, but we need to narrow the search more," Byte replied.

Peter tapped his finger against his chin, thinking. "Easy," he said after a moment. "We're still looking at *all* reported deaths, even the ones from natural causes. We need to specify the terms of Growler's probable death."

"Right." Byte typed in two more words for the computer to use in its search: **murder OR accident.**

This time, the computer worked for only a second or two.

Number of matches found................37

The Misfits looked at one another.

"It's still a large number, but we're much closer now," Jake said.

"Any ideas about how we can narrow it down from here?" Byte asked.

Mattie hauled himself onto the counter. He plopped down next to Byte's computer and stared at the screen, frowning. Jake played with his Superball as he pondered, tossing it just a few inches in the air. He didn't want to risk Ms. Langley's ire by bouncing it.

Peter grabbed a chair and scooted next to Byte. "You know what?" he said. "I was just thinking. Growler was in a lot of trouble, and the people who were after him were ruthless. If they were any good at finding people who owed them money—and I bet they were—maybe he didn't survive past 1957, the year he disappeared."

"Could it be that simple?" Mattie murmured.

"We can't count on it," admitted Peter.

"We can't count on any of this. But we can *try*," said Byte. She turned back to the keyboard and typed in a last command. **Date: 1957.** The computer's response came almost as soon as her finger bounced off the return key.

Number of matches found................3

Byte's fingers tingled as she lifted them from the keyboard. "I don't know what we've got here," she said quietly, "but we've got *something*."

They called up the articles one by one. The first referred to a black man in his late fifties who weighed over three hundred pounds. His body had been found in an alley, riddled with bullets. Police had been unable to identify him.

"Too old," said Peter, "and too big. We've seen pictures of Growler. He didn't weigh that much in 1957."

"Not unless he *ate* all those bonds," Mattie joked.

Peter glared at him.

"Sorry," Mattie said. "Gee, you used to have a sense of humor."

The second article referred to a teenager who had died in a knife fight in a bar. The teen had joined the merchant marine, having lied about his name and age so he could do so earlier than the law allowed. According to the article, the investigators went as far as proving that the victim was not who he said he was, but they never determined the teen's real identity.

"Scratch number two," said Mattie. "Too young."

Byte scanned the last of the three articles. "This one isn't much more than a series of gruesome facts." She took a deep breath. "'Victim appeared to be in his early thirties.' That's about the right age. Let's see, he died as a result of a fall from the roof of a hotel. Police found evidence of a struggle on the rooftop, so they believe someone pushed him." Byte felt the others waiting as she looked at the screen, swallowed, and finished reading the next sentence. "Listen to this… 'the victim's face was battered, apparently with a blunt instrument of some kind. No identification possible, even through dental records.'" Byte felt an odd tingling along her back, and she shifted uncomfortably in her chair. "And guys," she added, her voice almost a whisper, "the body didn't have any fingertips."

"What?" asked Jake.

"Yeah," she repeated, "it says so right here. The killer chopped off this guy's fingertips—just the tips, on both hands."

Peter nodded. "Whoever did this," he whispered, "didn't want anyone to identify the body. No face. No fingertips. No *fingerprints*."

A long silence followed. They all stared at the screen, and Mattie reached out and touched the monitor with his finger. "And look at this," he said. "Check out the name of the hotel where he died. It was called the Regal Arms."

"*Arms?*" asked Jake. "Whoah. 'Where lovers meet with open Arms.'"

Peter nodded. "Guys," he said, "I think we've found Growler Morton."

When school let out for the day, the Misfits decided to pay another visit to Helen Morton, knowing that only she could provide the answers they needed.

Byte sat next to Jake in the back seat of Peters Volkswagen. She was speaking to Peter, but her attention, Peter noted, was clearly on Jake. "I think Jake should ask the questions," she suggested.

Jake's eyes widened. "Why me?"

"She liked you," said Byte. "I could tell."

Peter agreed. "If that's true," he said, "she might be more comfortable answering the questions if you asked them. That means you're elected."

"Aw, *geez*...." Jake scrabbled for his schoolbooks and yanked out a sheet of paper. "Okay, okay," he said. "What do I ask?"

"Start with this...." Peter began.

They roared along, the convertible's top down and the wind whipping through their hair. Mattie occupied himself by holding his flattened hand outside the confines of the car and feeling the wind push against it.

Peter, after offering a few suggestions to Jake, found he could no longer concentrate. He glanced at Byte in the rearview mirror, watching the odd way she brushed at her hair as it flew about her face. She turned and looked at Jake, then began adjusting the collar of his shirt where it had folded over on itself. She smoothed the fabric with her fingers, and Peter felt himself shrink inside.

"She's an amazing lady, Peter," Jake called from the back seat, still scribbling notes.

"Huh?" said Peter.

"Mrs. Morton. You're really going to be impressed with her."

From the passenger seat, Mattie gave Peter a little nudge. "Hey, Jake," he teased, "you really like this lady. You going to ask her to prom or something?"

Peter remained silent. He saw Jake's arm reach over the passenger seat and wrap around Mattie's neck. Jake's free hand formed a fist from which a single, pointed knuckle protruded. Jake scrubbed the knuckle back and forth, hard, across the top of Mattie's head.

"Ow! Awright!" shouted Mattie, laughing. "No more noogies. Ow! *Jake!*"

A more sensible voice came from over Peter's left shoulder. "No, really," said Byte. "The lady just has this, I don't know, this *presence*. Jake's right. You'll see."

Peter followed Jake's directions to the house and pulled into the long, cobblestone driveway.

The house was a large colonial, and Peter thought the manicured lawn and sculpted hedges gave it a sterile look. He pulled up in front and stopped the car.

Peter, like Jake, lived far from the wealthy, old part of the city. The land owned by his family was rough, hilly, and forested—full of crickets, katydids, and bees. The air there hummed. Here, at the Morton home, Peter heard only the distant rush of the freeway and the painters squabbling over where to place a ladder.

The house was…lonely.

Byte must have felt it too. "I know," she said, glancing at the enormous home. "Just wait till you meet the lady."

Jake knocked on the door. He heard footsteps tapping against the marble floor inside, followed by the faint sound of one voice calling to another. The door opened, and Scott Morton peered out. He looked first at Jake and Byte, then at the other Misfits, and his eyebrows arched.

"Oh, great," he muttered, one side of his mouth curling up in a half-smile. "Now they're multiplying."

He leaned against the door frame and used his foot to swing the door open wide. "Mother lectured me about being rude to her guests," he told them. "So—won't you please come in?" He waited a moment before stepping aside—sending the message that, in spite of his mother's wishes, the Misfits were not truly welcome—then motioned for them to follow him down the hallway.

Mrs. Morton was in the living room, squirting glass cleaner on the windows. A machine for polishing the floor rested in a corner. Jake thought the woman looked tired, but when the Misfits entered the room she stood up straight and squared her shoulders.

"Well," she said, "my friends, the detectives. Solve your mystery yet?" She eyed the purple shade of Jake's nose and cheekbones, but said nothing.

Jake looked at Peter and swallowed. On the way here, the Misfits had decided it would be best, at this point, not to reveal what they seemed to have learned about Growler's death. The results of their computer search were clearly important, but the Misfits had no proof, only a strong hunch. None of the Misfits believed that such an emotionally charged piece of information—a man's brutal murder!—should be tossed about lightly around the man's wife. They would tell Mrs. Morton everything, but they would do so when they *knew* everything.

"We're still working on it," Jake replied. "We were wondering if we could ask you a few more questions."

Helen Morton hesitated. She then sighed and gestured toward the couch. The Misfits sat, but she remained standing, her arms folded around her as if for protection.

Jake, a little flustered, fumbled at his shirt pocket and withdrew a pen and his folded sheet of notepaper so he could write down Mrs. Morton's answers.

"Um," he began, trying to make out his own squiggly handwriting, "can you tell us anything about a hotel called the Regal Arms?"

138   At the sound of the name, Mrs. Morton seemed to teeter a bit. She reached for the window frame to steady herself. "That's a name I haven't heard in a very long time," she said. "It's where Growler and I met. His band was hired to play in the ballroom, but they had no singer to front for them. I heard about the opportunity and auditioned. Growler and I...hit it off." She looked at Jake. "Later, we spent our honeymoon there."

"Mrs. Morton," said Jake, "where is the Regal Arms?"

"Hmmm? Oh—in Santa Teresa." She smiled almost apologetically. "We were young. Couldn't afford anything nicer." She looked at Byte, as though a female might better understand what she would say next. "Besides, it was kind of romantic."

Jake frowned. "Didn't Growler have his recording contract by that time?" he asked. "Wasn't he a big jazz star with RSA?"

"Hmph," said Mrs. Morton. "In those days RSA was nothing but a bunch of crooks. They released 'Whisper My Name' a few weeks after we were married, and the song was a huge success, but we sure didn't see any money from it. They did a lot of 'creative' bookkeeping to avoid paying us the royalties they owed." She shook her head. "Years passed before time—and society— caught up with what was happening to young recording acts. I finally found a lawyer willing to sue RSA. When the record company realized I was willing to go through it all again—all the accusations, the trashing of Growler's name *and* mine—they knew they would lose.

They settled before it ever went to trial." She waved her hand at the house around her. "This is what I have of 'Whisper My Name.' The settlement gave me enough money to buy this house. I've been living on a small annual stipend ever since then."

Jake looked at the others quizzically. Even Peter seemed confused; none of this made any sense.

"Wait a minute," Peter said. "I thought your husband and Franklin Bellows were close friends. Bellows told us so, and we also read it in one of the newspaper reports about your husband's disappearance."

Helen Morton laughed. "Franklin Bellows and Growler friends? Don't believe everything you hear and read, young man. Mr. Bellows will say whatever he needs to say to make himself look good. My husband and I never trusted him. In fact, we were looking to go with another label as soon as Growler's contract was up. Bellows knew it, too. He and Growler had a huge fight. Growler…punched him. That's how Bellows got that scar on his cheek, from my husband's ring."

"So Growler was planning to leave RSA," Jake whispered to himself. The idea seemed to hang over him like a fog. He had no idea what it meant.

"Yes," said Helen Morton. "And Bellows was furious about it. RSA had made good money off 'Whisper My Name,' which they would get to keep, but Growler was on the verge of becoming one of the great ones. Everyone knew it. RSA would lose a fortune to another label when he left."

Jake nodded—understanding, finally, how little the Misfits really knew.

Struggling to get back on track, he glanced once more at his list of questions. "Mrs. Morton," he said, "this is very important. You had a piece of original sheet music Growler wrote just before he disappeared. Did you auction it off? Do you know who bought it?"

Helen Morton stared at Jake. Her mouth opened slightly, as though she were about to answer the question, but then her lip trembled. She closed her eyes, and her shoulders began to shake. "Enough," she said, sniffling. "No more questions."

Byte interrupted. "I'm sorry, Mrs. Morton, it really is very important...."

Scott moved quickly to his mother's side and placed his arm around her. He glared at the Misfits. "You heard her. I'd like you to leave now."

"But—" said Jake.

"Now!"

As they turned to leave, Peter stopped and faced Mrs. Morton one last time. He had remained silent during the questioning, but Jake had noticed the way the muscles in Peter's jaw had shifted when Mrs. Morton spoke about the hotel and about Growler's relationship with RSA. The leader of the Misfits had been thinking.

"Mrs. Morton," Peter asked, *"please.* About your honeymoon. You didn't happen to stay in room number twenty-three at the Regal Arms, did you?"

The woman slowly turned in Peter's direction. She collected herself, wiping her fingers across the wetness on her cheek.

"Mother—" said Scott.

"It's all right." She gazed at Peter. "It was room number *one* twenty-three," she said. "How could you possibly know that?"

Peter nodded. "Of course," he said, but Jake had the feeling he wasn't talking to anyone but himself.

"Room number one twenty-three?" Byte asked.

They climbed into Peter's Volkswagen. Peter started the engine and circled the car around to exit the driveway.

"I should have seen it," he replied. "The other clue. '*One* must look in the *twenty-third* place.' Once it became clear that one clue referred to a hotel, I figured the other might refer to a specific *room* in the hotel. I just forgot that hotel room numbers don't start from one, they start from one hundred."

"Are we going to Santa Teresa, then?" asked Mattie.

Peter didn't answer right away. "Hmmm," he said, "that's a good question. Growler and Mrs. Morton are linked to the hotel, so we might find out something there. And it would be nice to get there before the thief finds out about it, if we can."

"So what's the problem?" asked Byte.

"The problem *is* the thief," said Peter. "Santa Teresa is an hour and a half away. A trip there would put us horribly out of position if he should make another move in Bugle Point. Another problem is the third clue—the sheet music. We don't know who has it or what it says. What if it offers information we haven't anticipated? What if it sends our investigation in an entirely different direction? Going to Santa Teresa now, before we have all the clues, could turn out to be a huge mistake."

"So what's the bottom line?" asked Mattie.

"Bottom line," said Peter, "is that we should probably wait. We know the meaning of two of the three clues Growler left. As far as we know, the thief has only one—and he may or may not have figured out what it means. We can afford to wait another day."

Jake leaned back in his seat and closed his eyes. "Sure," he said, yawning, "at least until the guy breaks into my house and murders me in my sleep."

Mattie nodded. "Oh, right. There's that, too."

"—There's that, too."

The kid's voice dissolved in a crackle of static. It was bad enough they were driving in an open-air ragtop; now they were pulling out of range. Derek Bellows twisted the gain knob on the small radio receiver, but the static only grew louder. *So much for today,* he thought.

A three o' clock meeting today had prevented Derek from leaving the RSA offices. He had hidden the small radio receiver in his desk drawer, and later, when the meeting ended, rushed back to give the unit a try. Before he could begin, he had to chase Agnes, the old secretary, out of his office. It was amazing how that woman managed to have her nose in the wrong place at every turn. "Where are you spending your afternoons?" she'd asked. He had shooed her away like the pest she was, and her eyes had narrowed evilly.

Finally, after closing and locking his office door, Derek threw on a set of headphones. He had been kicking himself for a couple of days that he hadn't coughed up another three hundred bucks for the recording equipment that went with the bug; he could have set it to tape any conversations he missed when he couldn't be listening. Oh, well. He hadn't known at the time what he might find out, and he couldn't really have the darn thing sitting on his desk at work, could he? As for today, he didn't really expect to hear anything, but the nosy group of teenagers had accommodated him by driving into town.

He had been right. He had been *soooo* right.

These teenagers—Derek counted at least four of them now—were after Growler's money. Correction—*Derek's* money. And they were far closer to finding it than he had even guessed.

But now Derek himself was sitting right in the back seat of that Volkswagen, in a manner of speaking, and these teen detectives had no idea he was there. He had already learned quite a bit. He now knew that Growler Morton had left three clues, and that these kids already had two of them. He also knew that someone else, a thief, was in on the chase.

Fine, Derek thought. He would stay in the background and let these kids conduct their little investigation. And he would listen in on every word. When they found the third clue, and when they went to this hotel in Santa Teresa, Derek would be there. Waiting.

"Wanna see me make a card disappear?" asked Mattie.

"I'm tired," said Jake.

"Hey—Peter!" Mattie said, turning to him.

"I'm *driving*, Mattie," Peter said.

Byte tapped Mattie on the shoulder. "You can show me your trick," she said.

Mattie riffled the deck sharply and slipped it back into its box. "I don't need your pity," he said, feigning offense. He made a show out of thumbing his nose at all of them. Byte gave him a light punch in the shoulder, then threw her arms around his neck in a quick hug. When she withdrew, Mattie grinned smugly and returned the wristwatch he had slipped off her arm.

After the excitement of the afternoon, Jake thought, the remainder of the day passed fairly slowly. Peter drove the Misfits back to the high school, where Jake picked up his Ford Escort. The rest of the evening was typical: Peter gave Mattie a lift home. Jake gave Byte a lift home. Jake ate dinner. Jake did homework. Jake tried to practice with his broken clarinet. Jake threw his broken clarinet against the bedroom wall. It was *that* kind of evening.

A little after ten o'clock, Jake fell onto his bed and grabbed his stereo headphones. He dropped a CD into his Discman—Charlie Parker, live with Dizzy Gillespie, 1945—and closed his eyes. The music lulled him to sleep. He didn't awaken until an hour later, when Bird slipped into an improvisational saxophone solo that tugged Jake back to wakefulness. Jake touched a button on his CD player and ran the music backwards for several seconds so he could hear the solo again.

He got out of bed and made sure his schoolbooks and homework were organized. Then he picked up the pieces to his clarinet—there were a few more now than there were supposed to be—and dropped them into the wastebasket. They clattered as they landed.

Jake stared down at the broken pieces in the trash and saw a booklet—the program for the Morton auction. Some time ago, Jake had crumpled it and tossed it in the trash. Now he fished it out of the basket and unfolded it, smoothing out the crinkles against the top of his desk. Within the booklet, he saw the list of all the items Helen Morton had offered for sale at her auction. He saw the antiques, the furniture, the silver—he even saw his missing clarinet and the stolen 45-rpm record. Everything was there. Everything…

Jake blinked. He read the list a second time, and then a third. When he finished, the booklet dropped from his fingers and landed on the floor.

It said nothing about sheet music.

What did that mean? Jake wondered. Mrs. Morton had become extremely upset when they'd asked her about it…the music must have meant a lot to her. Could she have lost the sheet music over the years? Could she have thrown it away? Unlikely. Jake had met Helen Morton; he had seen her eyes when she spoke of her husband. She would never be careless enough to lose that sheet music, nor cold enough to throw it away. No, the only answer was that Helen Morton still had it in her possession.

And if Jake could figure that out, the thief could too.

Mrs. Morton was in terrible danger.

Jake grabbed his phone and called information. The number for the Morton home was unlisted.

Okay, Jake thought, *what do I do now?*

His instincts told him to call the police. Jake checked his watch. It was eleven P.M. Decker would have gone home hours ago, and Jake couldn't imagine an easy way of explaining this situation to another officer and being taken seriously.

Jake was certain that Helen Morton had the sheet music, and even more certain that the thief would come after her. But he could not be sure that the thief would act tonight. He had only a suspicion, and as powerful as it was, it would not command the resources of the police department. He needed proof that the theft was coming, and all he had was a decent guess.

And it was too late to drag the other Misfits out of bed and out of their homes. Gathering the four of them— even if it were possible at this late hour—would take too long. Peter lived too far away. Mattie lived with his grandparents even farther away. Only Byte lived close enough that Jake might pick her up on the way in, but he already knew what her mom would say about *that* idea.

No, whatever Jake chose to do, he would have to do by himself.

Jake turned off his CD player. Other than his own breathing, he didn't hear a sound in the entire house. While he had dozed, his parents must have gone to bed.

Throughout his entire life, his parents had set rules, and the rules had never seemed all that unreasonable. Jake had not broken them except for a few minor instances, which his father sometimes joked about at family gatherings.

Once, when he was a middle-school band student, the clarinet huge and unfamiliar in his hands, he had stayed after school to practice a new piece. His parents had told him to take the bus home, and to hurry so he could mow the grass before dark. Mowing the grass was to be his way of earning the clarinet.

But the piece called to Jake. He played it in band class, and then he played it again after school for his teacher. The teacher left at 3:30, so Jake sat outside on the bleachers and continued to play. The afternoon football practice broke up, and the players went home. A custodian walked along the school building, locking every door. The air grew cool. The notes Jake played seemed to drift away on the breeze. He didn't notice the passing hours

148 until the sun turned into a giant orange fireball and began edging below the horizon.

A car came screeching into the parking lot around 5:30—his mother, home from work, had been terrified at having found the house empty. She stepped out of the car, ran to the bleachers, and wrapped her arms around him. She helped him pull the clarinet apart and set it in its case, laughing and crying as she did. A moment later, as she led him to the car, she hugged him again, kissed his forehead, and threatened the worst punishments imaginable.

Now, as Jake quietly slipped out of the house, he figured the clarinet incident would be nothing compared the trouble he was heading into tonight.

Peter ignored the first ringing of the telephone.

At nine o'clock he had thrown on his pajamas, fallen into bed, and lapsed into a dreamless sleep. Now, two hours later, the phone seemed very far away indeed. It rang a second time, and Peter's arm, with little or no help from his brain, flopped once like a dying fish as it stretched toward the bed table.

The third ring roused him just enough to make him cranky.

He grabbed the handset and set it on his pillow, resting his head against it so that the pillow alone held the phone against his ear.

"Hrmmm?" he said.

"Peter," a female voice said, "Sorry...I couldn't sleep. Did I wake you?"

Peter swallowed the dry taste in his mouth and tried again to speak. He managed to snort out, "Huh? Wha—? Byte?"

"Yeah, it's me," she said. "Thank God your dad didn't pick up. I just *had* to call you right away."

"You did?" Peter was suddenly glad this conversation was taking place over the phone; he was certain the smile spreading across his face looked positively dopey. "You had to call *me*?"

"Oh, I can't believe it. I really blew it, Peter. I should have found this days ago."

"Well...calm down. What are you talking about?"

He heard Byte tapping on her keyboard. "I'm e-mailing you with a link to the Web site now. You're not going to believe this. I was messing around online—couldn't sleep, right? And I found an article about the whole Growler Morton affair, everything they know *for sure* about what happened."

"Yeah?"

"So get this," Byte said. "One of the suspects was *Helen* Morton. The police arrested her; the DA almost indicted her."

Peter sat straight up in bed. Byte had just managed to awaken him fully. "You mean they thought she had stolen the bonds?"

"More than that, Peter. When Growler never returned,

they accused her of murdering him. They were just never able to prove it."

"They thought Mrs. Morton killed Growler?" Peter let that revelation simmer a moment. "Well," he said, "she certainly wasn't the person who decked Jake or beat up Mr. McCollum. So if she's in on it, who's working with her? Scott?"

"Maybe," Byte agreed. "But he doesn't fit the description of the thief. There'd need to be someone else too."

Peter groaned. "Now this really makes my brain go tilt."

Byte was silent a moment, and when she spoke again, her tone was quiet and subdued. "I really am sorry, Peter," she said. "What if Mrs. Morton *was* involved? We went to her house, told her what we were doing…"

Her voice trailed off. She didn't have to finish; Peter knew what she meant. If Helen Morton was indeed involved in Growler's murder, the Misfits had placed themselves in terrible danger by approaching her.

"I should have caught it sooner, Peter," Byte said.

Peter heard the disappointment in her voice—and he certainly knew how he would feel if he thought he had let the group down. "Hey," he said, "no harm done, right? You caught it soon enough."

Byte paused before answering. "Well—okay," she said. "Thanks. You always say the right thing."

Peter slowly sat up in bed, grinning. "Really? I guess that's why you called me, huh?" he asked.

"Ummm, yeah," Byte replied, hesitating. "I mean, that and the fact that you've got a phone right by your bed and your folks don't yell at me if I call you late."

"Oh," said Peter. He tried not to sigh too loudly. "Well, all right, then. Try to get some sleep, okay? We'll meet with Jake and Mattie first thing tomorrow to go over the details."

"Peter?" said Byte.

"Yeah?"

"I just hate this…I hope she didn't do it. I'd really come to admire her."

"Yeah," Peter said. "If it turns out she's involved, Jake's going to be really disappointed too."

Jake pulled into the driveway of the Morton home, the cobblestones thumping beneath the balding tires of his Escort, then pulled off the drive and into the shadows as he approached the house. He checked his watch; it was eleven-thirty. *Not bad*, he thought. The idea was to get to Helen Morton before the thief did, and Jake figured he was right on time. *Any self-respecting thief would wait until after midnight to commit a burglary*, he thought.

The house was dark, which should not have been surprising, but the darkness made Jake hesitate before getting out of his car. Just overhead, a full moon rose behind a thick cover of clouds. It gave the clouds a bluish pallor that filtered down across the house and lawn and made Jake's spine prickle. That same hazy blue light also fell across the single tree in the yard, causing the tree's branches to throw dark shadows against the outer walls of the Morton home. When a breeze came up, the shadows moved like the fingers of a hand. Watching it, Jake swallowed, drew in a deep breath for courage, and stepped from his car.

He had been so concerned about getting to Mrs. Morton right away that he had not really thought about what he might say to her when she opened the door. Surely she would be frightened by the sound of the doorbell ringing at this hour, and even more frightened to see Jake, whom she hardly knew. What could he tell her within the first five seconds that would get her to listen to the whole story?

As he crept toward the double doors at the front of house, a dry, papery rustle came from a cluster of bushes nearby. Jake caught himself, spinning around at the unexpected noise. His eyes searched the bushes for—what? A pair of glowing eyes looking back at him? He chuckled at his edginess. *Just a breeze,* he told himself, and he repeated the thought just so he'd believe it. *Just a breeze.* But then he realized that if a breeze had caused the bush to rustle, it had not ruffled his hair, touched the leaves in the tree, or set Mrs. Morton's wind chimes in motion.

Jake stepped away from the door and into the shadows.

Someone was out there. Jake's mouth went dry and his heart began to pound. His mind screamed at him.

Think! Think! The way he had driven in here, with his lights on, his tires making that galumphing noise against the cobblestones—he had little doubt that anyone hiding in the bushes knew he was here. *Why didn't I think of that before?* he moaned to himself.

The bushes rustled again, and Jake began thinking he shouldn't have come at all. He should have called the police, or waited until tomorrow, or done any one of a number of things that would have occurred to a *sensible* person.

In the dark, he ran to the front door and began pounding on it. He glanced over his shoulder. Two seconds passed, and he pounded on the door again. *Come on! Come on!*

The wood was heavy oak, and the sound probably did not carry well in the large house. Just as Jake thought to search for a doorbell, another sound came to him, footsteps cracking dried twigs, and Jake panicked. But even through the panic, he knew he could not leave Mrs. Morton alone, in the dark, to handle this intruder, so he tore around to the side of the house. He remembered from the auction that Mrs. Morton had a fenced-in backyard. The fence was probably eight feet tall, but Jake knew he could scale it.

It materialized before him, a gray wall that seemed to loom out of the darkness and plant itself in his path. Jake never missed a stride. He jumped, caught the upper edge of the fence with his fingers, and was over. One foot landed on a large stone, and Jake sprawled in the dirt, grimacing at a sudden explosion of pain in his ankle. He hauled himself to his feet and listened. He couldn't hear any movement now, no rustling of leaves or footsteps crunching the gravel. All he could hear was his own tortured breathing and the grunts that burst from him every time he planted his injured foot.

He stumbled toward the glass patio door and pounded on it. The door rattled, but the glass was tempered and the lock strong; no matter how hard he pulled, he could not force it open. He pounded again, but decided he had waited here too long. The thief might reach him before Helen Morton got to the door. And then the thief would have *her* as well.

Dragging himself away from the patio, he continued circling the house. Perhaps, he thought, if he kept moving but remained quiet, the thief might lose track of where he was and grow nervous. Or perhaps Jake's pounding on the doors had already frightened the thief away. He waited, hoping a plan would just leap into his mind, but none came. Eerie blue shadows played across the house as the moon drifted behind wispy clouds. The panic welled inside him again.

At a loss, he staggered to the opposite side of the house and once more came upon the fence. This time he climbed it gingerly, slipping over and letting himself hang an instant before dropping the last few inches to the ground. He absorbed most of the impact on his good leg, steadying himself by gripping the handle on the gate.

Jake was breathing harder now, not from physical exertion, but from the anxiety of knowing that he was stalking someone—someone who might be only yards away. And that someone was stalking him as well.

Jake crept alongside the sculpted bushes that lined this side of the house, careful not to disturb so much as a leaf. He moved slowly—now breathing in, now holding his breath, now letting it out. Clouds drifted in front of the moon, and Jake felt safe, wrapped in the blackness.

A nearby cricket broke the silence, its rhythmic thrum loud and startling, like the sudden gunning of a dirt-bike's engine. Jake thought he heard a single footstep ahead, but he couldn't be certain. Once again he slipped into the shadows, waiting for another sound—the crack of a twig or rustle of a leaf.

He felt safe for a moment—until a figure dove from a nearby bush and slammed into him. A fist swept in a tight arc and connected with his jaw.

Jake's head snapped back. The figure drove a shoulder into Jake's midsection and wrapped its arms around Jake's knees. The two hit the ground, tumbling together down a grassy bank. When they stopped, Jake's assailant was on top of him, throwing wild, angry punches the way a child might after one too many run-ins with the neighborhood bully. Jake covered himself, and the punches bounced off his shoulders and forearms. The attack seemed to have no focus. If the man's intent was to hurt Jake, he had a long way to go before he accomplished that goal. Jake could lie there for an hour, letting the punches ricochet here and there harmlessly until the attacker exhausted himself. But after a few more seconds of this, Jake lost patience. His attacker stopped punching for an instant to catch his breath, and Jake was ready. He drew his elbow back and threw a single punch that landed across the man's jaw and sent him sprawling. Jake was up in an instant. He landed on top of the man and drew his arm back for another shot.

But now, with the attacker helpless beneath him and the moonlight casting its blue glow on the man's face, Jake finally understood what was happening. The man looked up at him, his arms raised to ward off Jake's next blow, his eyes wide and terror-stricken.

It was Scott Morton.

Jake blinked. "*Scott?*"

"Shhhhhh…. Don't hit me again," Scott said in a choked voice. Jake struggled to his feet, then helped Scott to his feet as well.

"Sorry," hissed Jake, "but you hit me first."

Scott opened his mouth wide, testing his sore jaw, then glared at Jake. "What are you doing here, anyway?"

Jake drew in a deep breath, then nodded at the house. "I—I thought your mom might be in trouble," he said quietly. "I came to warn her—it's a long story."

Scott continued to glare at him.

"But wait a minute," said Jake. "What are *you* doing here at this hour? You don't live here, do you?"

Scott shook his head. "No. Mom called me and asked me to come over and have a look around. She said she heard someone prowling around outside the house."

Jake glanced at the woods and shadows surrounding the grounds. "Why didn't she just call the police?" he murmured.

Scott didn't answer right away. He studied Jake for a few moments. "All right," he finally whispered. "Back—well, back when things happened forty years ago, Mom had some trouble with the police. They thought my dad was guilty of stealing the bonds, and they assumed she was in on the theft too—that she might have even murdered him. Dad was black, she was black, the money was gone. For them, it was a natural conclusion. Mom hasn't trusted the police since."

Jake nodded. But then his mind did a quick somersault. Something else Scott had said suddenly seemed far more important.

"Hold on," said Jake. "Your mother heard a prowler? How long ago did she call you?"

Scott shrugged. "About twenty minutes."

"I've been here for less than ten," said Jake. A breeze blew through the trees, and the rustling of the bushes and the tinkling of the wind chimes made him shiver. Every moving shadow, every stray sound, seemed to be an echo of someone's footsteps.

"We better get inside," Jake whispered. "He's here."

The night-vision goggles were working perfectly. Karl Logan had been scouting the Morton home for over two hours now, the goggles providing him with an eerie sort of daylight. They worked by magnifying light within a limited part of the spectrum. The result was a clear image that glowed in only one bright color. To Karl, it looked as though the entire Morton home were lit by stadium lights—and all the bulbs in the light fixtures were green.

He had seen Scott Morton arrive, and he had watched, concerned, as Scott wandered around the outside of the premises. The man's arrival was not at all helpful, and it was clearly not a coincidence. Logan didn't like it.

Logan was concerned that he may have crossed the line between overconfidence and carelessness tonight. Certain that the Morton woman was asleep, he may have taken one step just a little too loudly, or his shadow may have flickered past the wrong window, or the moon may have been just a little too bright. In any event, something had frightened the woman, and she had called her son.

Even more interesting, Logan thought, was the arrival of the teenager. It was the Armstrong kid. He recognized Jake immediately. Logan wasn't sure what conclusions the kid had drawn, but it seemed possible that the teen had noticed some sort of pattern developing in the thefts. Armstrong had shown up here on the very night Logan was hoping to steal the sheet music. His arrival, like Scott Morton's, was no coincidence.

Logan had seen the teenager speeding up the driveway in his car, and he had watched with some amusement as Jake and Scott Morton went tumbling through the grass. He was less amused when the two began talking and went into the house together.

He considered his options. If these two suspected he was planning to steal the sheet music tonight, then the risks of carrying out that plan had just multiplied. Logan's inner alarm system told him that he should leave this place and hole up in his hotel room, let tonight's tensions play themselves out. He could plan another approach later.

And yet, failing to attack now, while he was on site and prepared, carried its own risks. If Helen Morton had the sheet music, and she found out that someone was *after* the sheet music—a likely possibility, Logan thought, considering Jake Armstrong's arrival here tonight—then the entire job was in danger. The Morton woman could skip town, forcing Logan to track her down. She could hide the sheet music—or even destroy it, if she thought her life were in danger. The bottom line was, Helen Morton might now be in a position to cripple Logan's chances of completing this job.

He would have to act *now*—in the next few minutes. He would give the people inside the house no time to plan a defense. The only positive aspect of tonight's events was the fact that these amateurs had arrived instead of the police. To Karl, Jake's and Scott's bumbling suggested that Helen Morton did not think she was in much danger.

She was wrong.

He had parked his van through the woods and down the road behind some trees. As he jogged to it and pulled the necessary tools from the van's storage boxes, he thought about Jake Armstrong showing up just in time for Karl's theft of the music. Few law enforcement agencies had ever anticipated the thief's movements so well. Furthermore, Armstrong had flattened Scott Morton with a single punch. Karl was beginning to think he might have underestimated this teenager.

And he didn't like that one bit.

Logan followed his basic procedure: He tightened the harness of his shoulder holster and rechecked the ammo clip in his Colt. He fastened his leather tool belt around his waist. Satisfied, he then attached his climbing rope to the belt, having gone over every inch of it earlier, checking it for spots that were worn or frayed. Next, he hung the night-vision goggles around his neck so he could get to them quickly, and, finally, he pulled the ski mask down over his face.

He was ready.

Logan closed his eyes and took a moment to center himself. This simple exercise was perhaps the most important of his preparations. It calmed him and honed his concentration.

When he had conducted his study of the house earlier, Logan had noted the pattern of lights going on and off within. This was a shorthand method of determining the habits of the people who lived inside the house. Earlier, virtually every light in the Morton home had been burning. To Logan, that suggested that Helen Morton was an active woman; she was likely moving constantly about the house, leaving lights burning as she went. Now, though Scott Morton and Jake Armstrong had entered the house, it remained dark. Surely they were planning something. Logan smiled. Perhaps they were crouching in the dark, waiting for Logan to make a mistake. *Well, let them,* he thought. He would avoid them altogether. Morton and Armstrong would expect him to enter through a first-floor window. Instead, Logan would make his approach from above.

Putting on the night-vision goggles, Logan tossed a rubber-coated grappling hook toward the home's brick chimney—not to the eaves, where it would make more noise grabbing hold. Dangling from this hook was a climbing rope. Logan grabbed the rope, tugged at it to make sure that the hook had indeed taken hold, then scaled the side of the house until he came to a second-story bedroom window. Hanging from the home's outer wall, he reached into a pouch on his belt and removed a special tool he had devised—a motorcycle's side mirror welded to a folding twenty-four inch, jointed steel arm. Logan held the mirror to the window, gazing into it as he angled the arm back and forth. *Good.* The bedroom was unoccupied—indeed, it was completely empty. *And there's no alarm system.*

162   Logan folded the mirror then pulled another small device from his belt, one that consisted of a plastic handle, a button, and a rubber suction cup. He held the suction cup against the windowpane and pushed the button seven or eight times, creating a vacuum that drew the suction cup tightly against the glass. Next he took a glass cutter and drew a neat circle in the window itself. He gripped the plastic handle of his device, gave a little tug, and the circle of glass came away with the suction cup, leaving a softball-sized hole in the window. No screen blocked his entry. Logan simply reached in, gave the lock a twist, and in a moment was inside the room.

Getting into the house had taken less than thirty seconds.

He crept to the door of the room. In the absence of moonlight, it was now time to put on the night-vision goggles. He could see that he was at the top of a staircase, looking down a wooden stairwell that glowed a dull green. Logan moved slowly. The house was old, and the stairs undoubtedly creaked. He made his way down them, stepping near the sides of the stairs to avoid the worn, creaky centers. In a few moments he found himself in a den, surrounded by empty bookshelves, stacked cardboard boxes, and scattered pieces of furniture.

Of course. Helen Morton is moving. While staking out the house, Logan's guess had been that the manuscript pages, as treasured as they must be, would have a prominent place in the home. Perhaps he would find them framed and displayed on a wall, or stored away in a hope chest. Easy to find; easy to steal. With the move, however, his job became more difficult. If he were unable to locate the pages of music, he would just have to wake up the Morton woman and force her at gun-point to give it to him.

And there was still the matter of the two male party crashers. Where were they? Logan listened, but he heard no conversation, no footsteps moving through the house. A powerful rush of adrenaline coursed through him, and he stopped to listen to his own internal warn-ing system. *Calm. Peace. Confidence, not over-confidence. Don't betray your presence unless the situation requires you to do so.*

Logan took another step, and the "situation" suddenly became very clear to him. Just then, from behind a chair, a male voice whispered a single word.

"*Now!*"

Someone hit a light switch, and Logan's field of vision exploded. The night-vision goggles, designed to gather even the dimmest sources of light and magnify them thousands of times, blinded Logan in the fully illumi-nated room. The shock drove down his optic nerves and almost threw him into unconsciousness. He tore off the goggles and pressed his palms down on his closed eye-lids. He saw a green cloud, bright, glowing, floating against a black background.

Scott turned on the lights, and Jake froze, fascinated by what he was seeing. The man in front of him—dressed in black, wearing a ski mask, tool belt, gloves, and a gun at his shoulder—was reeling in pain. Jake wasn't sure what he and Scott had done to the man, but he very quickly saw how they could take advantage of it.

Scott and Jake leaped from their hiding places and tackled the intruder.

The thief slammed into the wall, but Jake knew right away that he and Scott hadn't hit him hard enough. The guy stayed on his feet, though his breath had been torn from his lungs, and Jake was certain an average man would have crumpled. Worse, although Jake wasn't sure what he and Scott had done to the man, he sensed that the thief was already recovering from his disorientation. Jake tried to pin down the man's arms, and he watched in horror as the brown eyes behind the ski mask fixed on him. Little crinkles formed at the corners of the eyes. The guy was *smiling*.

The thief made a little circular motion with his arms—as though they were shoelaces untying—and Jake's hold was broken. Now *his* arms were pinned. The thief spun him around easily, and Jake felt a boot pressing into his lower back. The thief shoved, and Jake went sprawling.

Jake landed on the floor; when he looked up, he saw Scott Morton battling with the intruder. Scott had managed to wrap his arms around the guy's legs. He was apparently trying to knock the man to the floor, where he and Jake could pin him down completely. The man gripped Scott's head in his large, gloved hands and slowly turned it, twisting Scott's neck. A rough flick of his arms sent Scott sprawling.

And then the thief must have decided that he had no more time to waste. For at that moment, in a move terrifying in its swiftness, he drew his gun.

The barrel of the gun moved steadily back and forth, swinging first toward Jake, then toward Scott. The air in the room seemed to crackle. Jake felt it. He looked again at the armed man before him and saw the tension there as well. The eyes behind the mask flickered back and forth across the room, taking measure of the space, looking for possible weapons, looking for an escape.

Jake sensed movement behind him.

"Stop!" a woman's voice said.

The voice belonged to Helen Morton, and it drew all eyes in her direction. She stood in the doorway, dressed in her bathrobe, her command ringing out and causing everyone in the room to freeze. In addition, her own calm seemed to have a calming effect on everyone else. Scott's ragged breathing softened at the sound of her voice. Even the thief's shoulders, Jake thought, seemed to relax.

"What do you want?" she demanded.

"I think you know," the thief said. "A piece of original sheet music your late husband left. 'Waltz with Helen.'"

Without saying another word, Helen Morton walked over to a cedar chest and raised the lid. She fished around inside the chest, and a moment later withdrew a memory album. She paged through the album and pulled out several sheets of paper. Then, paying not the slightest attention to the gun pointing at her, she strode over to the thief and handed the sheets to him.

"There," she said, "that's all of it. Now please leave my home."

The thief silently rolled the pages into a cardboard tube he produced from his belt.

Just then, lights flickered outside, and Jake heard the distant rumble of a car moving over cobblestones. He turned his eyes away from the thief and coughed, hoping the sound would cover the noise from outside.

He was glad he and Scott had been able to convince Mrs. Morton to call the police.

The thief must have noted the sound as well, for that moment his eyes stopped their hesitant glancing about the room. He bent quickly, picked up the goggles he had dropped on the floor, and padded, catlike, to the nearest window.

Scott, during this time, had not moved. Jake looked at him now and was fearful for him. He could see that Scott's face had reddened, and that his cheeks were huffing in an almost childlike anger. He was shifting his weight from one leg to another, like an animal about to spring. The thief had just raised the window. A growling sound escaped from Scott's throat, and he launched himself at the man.

"Scott, no!" shouted Jake.

The thief spun and delivered a kick that caught Scott on the side of the head. Mrs. Morton screamed. Scott fell, but he circled his arms around one of his attacker's legs. The thief kicked with the leg, trying to free it.

The car outside stopped rumbling. Doors slammed.

The thief took his gun, cocked it, and fired a single bullet into Scott Morton's leg. Jake winced at the gun's report and stared in odd fascination at the way the blood blossomed across the leg and rose through the fabric of Scott's jeans. The thief stepped through the window, first one leg then the other, and was gone.

Jake and Helen Morton ran over to Scott, who was clutching at the wound to slow the bleeding. Jake tore off his jacket and bound it like a bandage around the wound. Scott was staring helplessly at the open window and billowing curtains.

"You idiot," said Jake.

chapter nine

Thursday

Police Lieutenant Marvin Decker whispered quietly into the pay phone in the police department lobby.

By sneaking around a little, Decker was finally getting those ballet tickets without his partner, Sam, finding out. His wife would be happy, and Decker had avoided Sam's razzing. Not a bad start to the day.

He headed back to his office and found Sam waiting for him.

"Marv," said Sam, "I've got something. You're going to be very interested in this." Sam rustled the sheet of notes in his hand. "Okay. Last night a black male in his early forties showed up at the emergency room with a bullet wound to the lower leg."

Decker shrugged, sinking into his chair. "So turn it over to general investigations."

"Wait," said Sam, "I haven't gotten to the good part yet. The shooting took place at the home of Helen Morton."

Decker sat up straight. The Armstrong kid had purchased his stolen clarinet from the Morton auction.

Yesterday, he and Sam had taken a robbery report from an antique dealer whose purchase at the auction had also been stolen.

"The victim was Mrs. Morton's son, Scott," Sam went on. "He was shot during a burglary. The suspect stole nothing but the original manuscript to some sheet music written in 1957 by Jerome 'Growler' Morton." Sam raised his eyebrows. "Now do I have your attention?"

Decker pointed to the telephone. "Get Helen Morton on the line," he said. "I want to talk to her." It seemed clear now that the three separate incidents were related. Those kids—the Misfits—had mentioned something about finding a note inside the clarinet Jake bought. Decker also remembered that the theft report had mentioned a note connected with the record stolen from the antique shop. Something bigger than petty theft was happening, and robbery division would now take over from the uniforms and combine the three investigations into one.

"Already spoke to her," said Sam. "She's happy to talk with us, but she wants us to wait until her son gets home from the hospital later today."

"Hmph," Decker said. He didn't like that answer, but he figured he could live with it.

That afternoon, Decker and Sam drove down the cobblestone driveway leading to the Morton home. The first thing Decker noticed was the cherry red '67 VW convertible sitting in the driveway.

170 "You know what, Sam?" he said, sighing, as he and Sam got out of the car. "Nothing about these kids surprises me anymore. Sometimes it seems like the Misfits have been in my hair forever. In fact," he grumbled, "I'm beginning to think that if I were to flip through a book of photos from the day President Kennedy was assassinated, I'd find these four kids peering over the grassy knoll for clues." He shook his head.

Decker rang the doorbell.

"Sit down!" ordered a woman's voice from inside the house.

Decker and Sam looked at each other in surprise.

"I can get it, Mother," replied a man. "I'm not paralyzed, for Pete's sake."

A moment later, the door swung open to reveal a black man—no doubt Scott Morton—leaning in the doorway. Morton wore a pair of old jeans, one leg of which was cut open from the cuff to the knee. A heavy bandage encircled his calf and ankle. Decker also noted the bruising along Morton's jawline, where it appeared that someone had delivered a good, solid punch.

Decker handed him a card. "Good afternoon, Mr. Morton," he said. "I'm Lieutenant Decker." Then, indicating Sam, he added, "and this is Lieutenant Pappas. Glad to see you're on your feet."

Scott Morton smiled and indicated the crutches. "Yes," he said, "all three of them. Come on in."

He led them down a long hallway and into a living room where a few pieces of furniture and sealed cardboard boxes lay scattered. An attractive woman in her late sixties sat on the sofa. The woman, though seated, looked stiff and oddly uncomfortable at the sight of Decker and Sam. The two detectives introduced themselves and shook hands with her. Decker sat down and flipped open a palm-sized spiral notebook.

"Let's start from the beginning," he said.

The story unfolded quickly. Decker took notes, while Sam stood quietly across the room speaking with Scott.

"Mrs. Morton," said Decker, after he had heard the details of the break-in, "three times this week, a theft report about an item relating to you or to your late husband has crossed my desk. My primary concern now is that there appears to have been an escalation of violence with each theft. The first involved a man attacking a teenager; the second involved an assault on an antique dealer. The most recent theft, of course, resulted in the shooting of your son. You understand my concern. There is only one place for the violence to go now, and I do not care to see that happen. Is there anything else you can tell me—beyond what I've seen in the original reports—about these items or about last night? Anything that might lead us to the thief?"

Helen Morton looked at her son, and her son looked at one of the teenagers—Jake Armstrong. The teenager looked at his friends, and one of them, Peter Braddock, cleared his throat.

"Um, Lieutenant," said Peter, "We may be able to help you with that."

172   Peter knew that Decker was aware of the clues—the ones from the clarinet and the record sleeve—because the Misfits had told him about them when they first suspected the thief might be one man. But perhaps the lieutenant, in focusing on the thefts and the violence, had not considered the importance of the forty-year-old mystery of Growler Morton. The Misfits would have to detail for him the work they had done.

Byte produced her computer printout of the news photo of the three items on the bed table. Peter told Decker how the Misfits had tracked down the antique dealer. Mattie, eagerly interrupting, told Decker what they had learned at RSA. Finally, Jake explained how he had guessed that the thief would come to the Morton home, and how the Misfits had returned today out of concern for Scott.

"Anything else?" Decker asked.

Peter and Byte threw guilty looks at each other. In the light of last night's events, their suspicions of Helen Morton seemed almost silly. Neither would speak of those suspicions to the lieutenant.

"Good," said Decker, scribbling. The report filed by the uniformed officers had included little information beyond details of the shooting, the item stolen, and its approximate value. The Armstrong kid's explanation about the connection between the three thefts had received only casual mention. Decker would have to have a word with the officer who had filed the report. "So if your theory is correct," Decker went on, "then our little crime wave may be over. Your thief has stolen all three items."

Jake shook his head. "Not exactly, Lieutenant. Remember? The thief got my clarinet, but he never got the note that was inside."

Listening to Jake, Peter felt a stab of guilt for his earlier twinges of jealousy about Jake and Byte. His friend was in real trouble.

"So," added Jake, "I guess I'm still a target."

"We'll get him," said the lieutenant. "Can you identify the guy who was here last night?"

Jake shrugged helplessly. "He was wearing a mask." He went on to describe the thief's general size and build—and his brown eyes, admitting that he might have worn another set of tinted contacts.

Decker nodded. "I'd like to see that slip of paper from the clarinet," he said. Then he turned to Sam and closed his notebook. "Sam, let's put a watch on the Armstrong home. I want a black and white to swing by every half hour or so."

Sam nodded. "I'll radio for it as soon as we get back to the car."

"Jake," Decker continued, "I don't really think your thief is going to show up again. He's committed assault with a deadly weapon, and he has to know we're onto him now. He's smart enough to know what will happen to him if he's caught." He paused, then drew in a deep breath. "But," he went on, "the guy who broke in here outran three of our best—and fastest—young officers last night."

"Lieutenant," Peter offered, "the use of disguises suggests that the man is a professional. Which also suggests a man who is businesslike and…" He glanced at Jake, dreading what he was about to say, but deciding he needed to say it anyway, "well, possibly cold-blooded… about his work."

Decker nodded slowly. "Right," he agreed. "We won't take any chances. I'll do some checking—go through some FBI and Interpol files to see what I come up with. Don't worry. We'll catch this guy."

With that, Decker nodded his good-byes, and he and Sam left.

Peter continued mulling over what he knew of the thief. Such a man, he believed, wouldn't think twice about eliminating witnesses like Jake and Scott. He stared at the bandage around Scott's leg.

Jake walked over to Scott and sat next to him.

"You're lucky," said Jake, "that he didn't kill you."

Scott nodded. "I know."

"Yeah," said Peter, finally giving voice to his thoughts. "I wonder why he didn't."

The others glared at him.

"Peter!" exclaimed Byte.

"No," he said, "it's just that, considering the circumstances, it is kind of strange, isn't it? I mean, look at it this way…." Peter rose and stood by the den window, which was now coated with sticky fingerprint dust. "I'm the thief. The police are banging at the door, coming to arrest me. I'm in a hurry. Mr. Morton is grabbing my leg, stopping me. Look where my hand with the gun is. Look where Mr. Morton's head would be. It's not like I could miss."

Byte crinkled her nose, setting her glasses a little straighter on her face. "Peter," she said, "this is not exactly an enjoyable subject, all right?"

"No, wait," said Mattie. "I see where Peter is going with this. Instead of just pointing the gun and shooting at the nearest target—sorry—Mr. Morton's head, the guy leaned way over and fired into Mr. Morton's leg."

"Mr. Morton's *lower* leg," added Peter. "The calf. Lots of muscle there. Probably less chance of serious injury than if he had shot Scott somewhere else. And remember—help was right at the door."

Scott Morton looked at him, his fingers absently rubbing a small bump on his head as he considered Peter's words. "I know I brought this on myself for jumping the guy," he said, "but you're saying that, even after I jumped him, the thief didn't want to hurt me? That he went out of his way to *avoid* hurting me?"

"Sure seems like it," said Peter. He found a chair and slumped down into it, his head lolling back, his eyes closed. "What kind of guy are we dealing with here?"

Karl Logan stood on the empty pier at the Bugle Point Marina. He stared out over the Pacific Ocean, thinking first of the beachfront home he loved, and then of a promise he had made to himself.

Years ago, when he had made the pact, he had anticipated this day. He would not have guessed that the end would come this soon, or that it would come at the hand of a teenager, but he had always known it would come. He had planned for it. Logan's Swiss bank accounts held millions, and no individual or law enforcement agency could track the funds or the person to whom those funds belonged. He had also prepared another identity, one he had falsely documented in perfect detail and had never used before.

He thought of the events of the previous night, replaying them in his mind, watching himself in slow motion as he entered the Morton home. He saw himself creep down the stairs. He heard the sound of his feet padding lightly on the den floor, the faint clicking of his tools against the leather belt, and the whispered command *now*. His eyes involuntarily closed as he remembered the explosion of light and his subsequent blindness. Most of all, Karl remembered the cold feel of his weapon as he drew it from his belt. He had acted quickly to disable his assailant, as his training taught him, and he had saved himself. Shooting Scott Morton in the leg provided Logan with an escape, and it did so with a minimal amount of collateral damage. That was business.

But it was a way of doing business that Karl Logan could not accept.

He gazed at the sun, at its rounded edge just touching the water as it began to set. God, how he loved that wide open expanse of sea and sky!

The issue he faced was not only one of morality, of course. It was practicality. Last night Logan, really for the first time, had found himself in a position where he was not in control. He had been able to rescue himself, but an element of luck had helped him along as well. Luck was not a dependable—or renewable—resource.

Somewhere along the line his planning had failed. Though he had captured the prize, his methods were lacking. As a result, he had made himself the target of a police investigation that was far more aggressive than the ones he usually faced. This afternoon, Logan had hacked into the local P.D.'s computer system. He had discovered files on all three of the Morton-related thefts. Most disturbing was the fact that all three reports, though signed by different uniformed officers, now appeared in a file under one detective's name—a lieutenant named Decker. Logan understood that his three thefts were now part of a single, coordinated investigation. Taken together, the thefts might be remotely traced to one of his false identities—compromising his ability to operate effectively in the future.

But of course, that matter was already settled. Shooting the gun had settled it.

He looked again at the ocean. The setting sun threw off tendrils of light that rippled on the water's surface.

It was time. Karl Logan stepped to the edge of the pier. His eyes followed the distant boats, their running lights cutting luminous paths through the water. He was alone. He saw no amateur fishermen tonight, sitting with their legs dangling over the edge of the pier, holding twenty-pound test line with bare fingers and sinking it into the water. It was cold, and tonight was a school night.

Logan reached into his jacket and withdrew his prized 1911 Colt. He looked at it one last time, running

178 his finger lovingly along the barrel, then let it drop into the ocean. Ripples formed when it struck the water, and they cascaded outward until Logan could no longer see them, could no longer tell where they went or how long they survived. Bubbles rose to the surface as the gun sank. Water was invading the weapon's insides and forcing out the air.

A wooden sign on the pier, weathered by the salt spray, indicated that the water here was twenty-eight feet deep. Karl knew the gun would sink until the sand at the bottom swallowed it up. Later, if some unlucky fisherman were to snag it with a line and drag it back to the surface, the saltwater and sand would have corroded it so thoroughly that the gun would not fire. Ballistics tests against the bullet from Scott Morton's leg would not be possible.

But Logan was not just here to destroy evidence. Tossing the gun aside was a symbolic act as well. Tonight he would double-check the foundations of his new life: his new identity and his foreign bank accounts.

He turned away from the pier and headed back to his van. Before he left Bugle Point, he had a few more things to take care of.

Logan went back to his hotel room to plan the last few steps of his final operation. He had turned over the message in the 45-rpm record to his client. The sheet music, with whatever message it might contain, was now in hand. All that remained was the message from the clarinet.

Before Karl Logan could retire, he would have to deal once again—and for the last time—with Jake Armstrong.

He booted up his laptop. When he discovered that his client had hidden information from him, Karl had insisted on receiving more money before completing the assignment. The client had agreed.

He accessed his bank, typed in his security code, and noted the most recent activity in his Swiss account. He saw the initial deposit his client had made by electronic transfer, but he found no additional deposits. That was strange. Karl looked again, scanning the information on his computer screen, but he found nothing.

So, now he and his client had *two* things to discuss.

Karl reached for his cell phone and dialed his client's number. It rang five times before someone picked up.

"Hello?" The voice sounded weak and raspy, as though the speaker were ill.

"It's me," said Logan. "We have to talk."

"Talk? You better believe we have to talk! Are you crazy? Do you know what you've done?"

Logan stiffened. "Is there a problem?"

"Yes, there's a problem!" hissed the voice. "The mess you made is all over the six o'clock news! I thought you would handle these thefts more…*quietly*. I thought they would be so small-time the media wouldn't be interested in covering them. Even the police would basically ignore them." The speaker paused. "But you *shot* a man."

"It was necessary," said Karl. He did not explain to his client what that choice had meant to him. The client would not have understood. "I have the sheet music. I can deliver it as scheduled. There is, however, the matter of our new contract agreement. You haven't made a payment."

"We *have* no contract," hissed the voice. "You voided the contract when your clumsy efforts dragged the police into this. They'll find you. And if they find you, it's possible they'll find me. My life will be ruined." Borderline hysteria tinged the voice. Logan heard the client drawing in several deep, calming breaths.

"Okay," the client said, seeming to settle down somewhat, "okay. Listen, forget the note from the clarinet. I have the 45. You have the sheet music. Even if one of the clues is still floating around out there, no one will be able to put all three together, so I should be safe. As for you, be happy you got paid half, considering how you've bungled this job. Just get out of town. I won't feel truly safe until you're gone."

Karl grunted. "I'm not accepting that," he said. "I've acquired the three items we contracted for. You've paid me only half my fee. I want the other half. By tomorrow. Or you may not like the consequences."

"Don't threaten me," the voice spat. "You won't kill me over a money matter, and short of killing me, you're out of options. If you…turn me in…I'll give you over to the police. So take your half, get on a plane, and be thankful. You're fired!"

The client hung up.

Karl Logan examined the client's argument. Had he indeed failed to honor his part of the contract? While it was true that the police were now involved, an investigation was a problem for Karl, not for the client. Karl

shook his head. No, he had stolen the three items as
promised; he saw no justification for accepting only half
his fee.

But what could he do about it?

He sat on the floor and once again settled into the
lotus position. He meditated, washing away the anger
and frustration that blocked his creativity, and waited
for an idea to come. When one did, he smiled to himself.
It would require his climbing equipment, and it would
probably take most of the night, but it would more than
satisfy Karl's desire for justice.

He thought for a while longer, and another idea came
to him as well. This one made him laugh aloud. It was
risky, but it was also too perfect to resist.

Jake did not arrive home until well after dark. His
muscles ached. He had endured a full day of school, a
trip to the Morton home to check up on Scott, and then
had to borrow another clarinet for the evening rehearsal
of the band's upcoming spring jazz concert.

Last night's events at the Morton home had been the
top story on the morning news broadcast, and though
the anchorman did not mention Jake by name, the
description of a "tall, muscular, BPHS junior," stolen
sheet music, and the late Growler Morton had certainly
made an impression at breakfast. Jake had spent twenty
minutes trying to talk his parents out of grounding him
for sneaking out of the house—and had failed miser-
ably. School and band practice only. For a month. His

efforts were not the least bit helped by the police squad car that had pulled into the driveway and the two uniformed officers who had come knocking at the door—just to let his folks know everything was "okay."

Now Jake dragged himself through the front door of his home. His folks were cuddled together on the couch, a blanket around their shoulders, pizza crusts strewn across plates on the coffee table, and the TV flickering a Tom Hanks–Meg Ryan movie.

"Hey," mumbled Jake.

"Hey there," his mom said. "We saved you some pizza in the fridge."

Jake waved off the offer. He dropped his backpack next to the table and yawned. Then he walked upstairs, thinking that crashing in bed and watching a movie on cable sounded better, even, than eating pizza. The door to his room was ajar. He pushed through it, tossing his jacket over a chair, and he was just about to kick off his shoes when the door slammed closed behind him. Jake spun toward the sound, and his legs very nearly collapsed beneath him.

Standing in the middle of the room was a tall, brown-haired man wearing Levis, a black T-shirt, and black leather gloves. The man smiled at Jake and stuck out his hand.

"Hello, Jake," he said. "I'm Karl Logan. We met the other night."

Logan did not appear to be armed, but Jake had seen enough to know it would be foolish to attack the man. Jake backed up against the wall and glanced at his bedside lamp and clock radio—useless as weapons against a trained fighter.

"The police are watching this place," Jake said.

Logan leaned casually against Jake's desk. He eyed Jake and crossed his arms. It was an odd gesture, Jake thought, for a man who might expect a fight from a powerfully built teenager. Then Jake realized that Logan saw the possibility of a fight, but was not the least bit concerned about it. "I know," replied the thief. "I'll be gone before they swing by again." He pointed toward Jake's bed. "Please, sit down. Relax. I'm not here to hurt you."

Swallowing hard, Jake sat. Logan radiated an intense aura of calm. It passed over Jake like warm bath water.

"You're not wearing a disguise," Jake said, "are you? I could identify you to the police."

"Call it a sign of respect," said the thief. "And don't worry. By the time you describe Karl Logan to the police, I'll be someone else."

"Look," said Jake, "if you want the note from my clarinet, it's there—underneath the stapler on my desk. Just take it and go."

Logan dismissed the idea with a wave of his hand. "Doesn't interest me anymore," he said. "In fact, I didn't come here to take anything. I came to give *you* something." Logan held up his left hand to show that he was holding a sheaf of papers. He leaned closer to hand them to Jake.

Jake instinctively pulled away, then reached for the papers. He stared at the sheets, disbelieving. They were the manuscript pages to "Waltz with Helen."

In spite of his fear, Jake felt the fingers of his free hand curling into an angry fist at the sight of the papers. "You *shot* a man for these last night," he said, almost shouting.

Logan held up his index finger. "No," he said. "No, I did not. I shot a man who was preventing my escape from the police. It was my freedom at stake, not those sheets of paper."

"But why are you bringing them to me?" Jake asked, glancing at the sheets to see that they were, indeed, the missing pages.

The man shrugged. "Let's just say I have a different agenda now. And I'm trusting you'll find a good use for those." He grinned, and then he touched his fingers to his forehead in a casual salute. "I'd better go," he said. "The police will be back in eleven and a half minutes, and I have something else to do tonight."

Logan moved toward Jake's bedroom window. He slid it open and swung first one leg over the sill, then the other.

"*Wait!*" said Jake. He stood rooted to the floor, but longed to take a single step forward, to stop the thief from leaving. Jake wanted his answers. "Who are you working with? What do the clues lead to? What happened to Growler Morton? Do you know what's going on? The whole story? *And where the heck is my clarinet?*"

But Karl Logan vanished in the dark without answering.

chapter
ten

Friday

ranklin Bellows felt particularly good this morning. As was his custom, he had awakened at five, put in an hour's workout at his club, followed it with a steam bath and a dip in the cold pool, then finished with a massage. For breakfast he ate a bran muffin and some fresh strawberries.

At 7:55 he entered his office suite at RSA Records, noting the red light burning on the small office coffeemaker. Excellent. Fresh coffee, a designer blend Bellows ordered from a coffeehouse in San Francisco— at sixteen dollars a pound—burbled inside. The aroma saturated the air, filling the office with the scent of French vanilla tinged with hazelnut. Bellows closed his eyes and savored the smell.

He greeted his secretary as he poured himself a large mugful of the brew. "Good morning, Margaret."

"Good morning, Mr. Bellows."

"Have Derek sent up in an hour or so, please."

"An hour, Mr. Bellows?"

"Yes," muttered Bellows, "I would think he's not likely to be later than that."

He went into his inner office and sat at his desk to review contracts and sales figures. Derek arrived at 9:15—out of breath and with tie askew, as though he had finished knotting it on his way up in the elevator. Derek had taken on the "fashionably unshaven" look, letting his beard grow out for a week or so before shaving and letting it grow out again. Perhaps that's how the models in men's fashion magazines looked, but Bellows wished his son would just shave daily and be done with it. Derek looked sloppy, and sloppy appearance made for sloppy work.

"Yes, Dad?"

Bellows pointed to the small chair across from his desk. "Sit." He rose and stood a few feet from his son, towering over him. "I received a phone call from Eagle Management. They're wondering why we haven't sent out the contracts for Razorwire."

Derek lowered his head and ran his fingers through his hair.

"*You* were responsible for mailing that contract," Bellows went on. "Fortunately, I was able to talk Razorwire's manager out of signing with another label."

His son remained silent, refusing to look at him.

"*What are you thinking?*" Bellows shouted. He waited for an answer, and when he received none, he reached down and yanked at his son's tie, straightening the knot.

"You're a mess! You've been coming in late most mornings—and slipping out during the afternoons." He drew his face close to his son's, forcing Derek to look at him. "Bottom line, Derek, you had better shape up and become a part of this team. The fact that you're my son is not a license to be a lazy fool. If you think it is, I'll toss you out of that office faster than I'd throw out a piece of rotten meat."

Franklin Bellows went to his desk and began looking through his morning paperwork. A moment passed, and Derek rose without saying a word. Bellows glanced at him, then went back to his work, vaguely hearing the office door clicking shut as Derek left.

An hour ago Bellows had been too full of thoughts of his son's failings to settle into his daily work routine. Now he rose and set the thermostat to the temperature he preferred—a cool sixty-two degrees, perfect for a trim businessman who favored wool suits.

Next Bellows raised the blinds to enjoy his twelfth-floor view of Bugle Point's downtown and marina. But what he saw was so odd, he found himself staring silently for several long moments, uncomprehending.

There, in the center of his window, was a clean, circular hole about the size of a beach ball. A breeze from the marina whispered through the opening, ruffling the executive's perfectly combed hair.

The coffee mug trembled in Bellows's hand. Warm, dark liquid sloshed over the mug's rim and splashed against his white dress shirt.

During the morning break, Jake grabbed Mattie and led him to a table in the school library. In two minutes, he laid out the events of the previous night in terrifying detail.

"I do not believe this," said Mattie. "I absolutely do not believe this story."

"Believe it," said Jake. "After the guy left, a muscle in my thigh started twitching, and it didn't stop until third period today. I've never been so scared in my life."

Last night, Jake could neither sleep nor bring himself to call the other Misfits, but by morning he had recovered somewhat. He thought about calling Lt. Decker, but he was afraid Decker might confiscate the sheet music as evidence, and he wanted the Misfits to see the music first. He decided he and his friends could drop the pages by Decker's office this afternoon, using school as their excuse for not producing them sooner. Jake figured they had about a fifty/fifty chance the lieutenant wouldn't chew their heads off.

"I'm mad you didn't call me," grumbled Mattie.

"Sorry," Jake said. "After this Logan guy left, I guess I was kind of in shock. I couldn't do anything, I couldn't even *think*. I just turned on the television and sprawled in front of it. I can't even remember what I watched."

"And you didn't tell your folks?" Mattie asked.

Jake frowned. "Well, I thought about that. But by then Logan was long gone, and I began to think that he really wasn't interested in hurting me or my folks. He seemed to be—well, enjoying himself. Like he was playing a joke on somebody. If I told Mom and Dad about him, they'd never sleep again."

"Hey, I wouldn't either, and I'm not the one who had a deadly, armed, criminal, black belt martial artist with absolutely no conscience shooting the breeze with me in my bedroom."

"Right, so I couldn't tell them. But I really don't think we're in danger."

Jake gazed out over the library floor. It seemed strange, he thought, to be trying to decipher a forty-year-old mystery—involving three million dollars and the disappearance of a man—while everyone around him was just struggling to solve a few math problems or write a rough draft of an essay.

Peter and Byte finally walked into the library together. Byte waved to Jake and Mattie from the doorway.

"We're in business," said Mattie.

Jake reached into his folder and withdrew the sheets of music. He spread them out on the table so everyone could see. "It looks pretty straightforward," he said to Peter. "I don't know what to make of it."

Peter glanced at the pages. "'Waltz with Helen.' I'm wondering why a jazz musician is writing a waltz to begin with. Isn't that a little weird?"

"Maybe that's the clue," said Byte.

It was a standard waltz, set in 3/4 time. Jake could hear the rhythm just by looking at the notes on the page— ONE two three, ONE two three.

"It's pretty simple," he told the others. "Basically three beats to a measure, mostly quarter notes, a few eighths here and there. Very pretty, but nothing a first-year band student couldn't play."

"Could Growler have hidden a message in the notes?" asked Peter.

Jake shook his head. "If he did, it would be like hiding a message in a basic arithmetic problem. There's no complexity here."

"Well," said Byte, "the other messages were written out, so maybe this one is too. Maybe the clue is hidden in the lyrics."

Jake gazed down at the words that Growler Morton had scrawled forty years ago in dark pencil. He had pressed so hard that the letters made angular impressions in the heavy paper. Once, where he had dotted an *i*, his pencil point had stabbed a tiny hole.

Beneath the moon we start to dance,
It's a lover's night, a lover's chance.
I tell her she's mine; I know that she knows,
Now I waltz with Helen where the cool breeze blows.

Some say there's a reason for every good-bye,
Some say there's a time when each lover must cry.
But tonight we hear music, and a full moon glows,
So I'll waltz with Helen where the cool breeze blows.

And if a time comes when her life seems unfair,
When the music plays, and I'm no longer there...

Then I'll reach down from heaven, and touch her sad heart,
And I'll gently remind her we never will part.
And I'll trust that she'll hear me and know where to go,
And I'll waltz with Helen where the cool breeze blows.

"That's it?" asked Byte.

Jake nodded.

"Well," said Peter, "it's definitely intended to mean something. Look at all these allusions to separation—a 'reason for every good-bye.' Lovers crying. There's even a suggestion that the speaker in the song is dead. He's 'no longer there'; he'll 'reach down from heaven.'"

"So you figured it out?" asked Mattie.

"Nah," said Peter, "not to my satisfaction, at least." He looked at Jake. "It does appear, however, that Growler Morton was not only planning to leave when he wrote this, he was also quite certain that he wasn't coming back. The lyrics about his death suggest he knew someone was trying to kill him."

"That's what I thought too," said Jake.

"*And I trust she'll hear me and know where to go,*" echoed Byte, looking at the others. "Suggests he was trying to lead Mrs. Morton somewhere. That's sad."

The four became silent. Peter stared once again at the sheets of paper. After several moments, he raised his head, looked at the others, and shrugged his shoulders. "I think," he said, "it's time for us to pay a visit to Santa Teresa. Maybe once we're inside room number one twenty-three at the Regal Arms, this last clue will explain itself."

Byte looked at Jake. "Aren't you grounded?"

Jake raised his hands helplessly. "I'll beg. I'll plead. I'll work it out."

"All *right*," cried Mattie. He did a little celebratory dance in his seat. "Come ooonnnn, girls! I may be short, but I'm a *millionaire*."

Derek Bellows sat in his Corvette. The receiver for the bug rested on the passenger seat next to him, its cord patched into the cigarette lighter jack on the dashboard. A loud hiss came through the car's stereo speakers. Bellows, still struggling with the equipment, adjusted the gain, and the hiss grew louder. He adjusted it again, and the static faded to a whisper of background noise.

He had parked his Corvette a little less than a mile from Bugle Point High School. This distance was well within the bug's range, and his location served as an effective stakeout point. If the teenagers decided to make a run for the interstate, Derek would know, and he would spot them as they passed by.

His fingers tapped a rhythm against the steering wheel. Heavy metal music rang in Derek's head. He hummed, and his mind translated the sound to guitar on full distortion.

A few minutes after three o'clock, a series of clicks emanated from his car's stereo speakers. Derek recognized the sound as the door locks on Peter Braddock's Volkswagen. The microphone was working. He heard the car doors open, and a young male voice shouted, "I get shotgun."

It was the little kid, Derek decided. The one named Mattie.

The Volkswagen's engine roared to life, and Derek had to turn down the volume.

"Did you instant message your mom?" asked another male voice.

"Yes," responded a female. "She wasn't crazy about my going so far, but she said okay."

"Peter, do you know how to get to the hotel?" someone asked.

"Not exactly," came the reply. "I called the Chamber of Commerce, but I got someone who hadn't worked there very long. He said that he thought the Regal Arms might have changed names. We can ask for help finding it when we get there."

Derek drummed his fingers even harder. *So*, he thought, *they're finally going to Santa Teresa*. They had talked about needing a third clue; they must have found it. Derek waited several moments, then, with the car still in park, gunned the Corvette's engine. Even in a clunky VW, it shouldn't take too long for those kids to pass him, and he wanted to be ready.

Three minutes later, he saw the car.

Derek swung his Corvette out of the parking lot and made a left turn onto the street. The red Volkswagen was two car lengths ahead of him.

194   As he drove, he turned on the stereo, and the music sounded very much like the song he had been hearing in his head—Nirvana's "Smells Like Teen Spirit." His life was an action film, and his stereo was playing the soundtrack. He stepped on the accelerator, and the music echoed the scream of the Corvette's engine.

"Here's where we start," said Peter.

The Misfits had arrived in Santa Teresa. Peter drove through the downtown area, growing impatient as he struggled to find a parking space. He finally pulled in front of a dry cleaners, just slipping into a spot as another car backed out. He ignored the sign that said "Parking for Axis Cleaners Only."

At least they had found the right area of town, Peter thought. Santa Teresa catered to a large number of tourists each summer, and the city had set aside a certain part of town as a "hotel district." Every hotel in the city clustered in this area, which lay within blocks of Santa Teresa's touristy shops, restaurants, and beaches. The Misfits remained in Peter's car, scanning the distant string of neon signs. Holiday Inn, Comfort Inn, Marriott, Ramada. They counted over a dozen.

But they saw no hotel called the Regal Arms.

"Well, there's a zillion people walking around," said Mattie. "Let's just ask somebody." He called out to a young man who was rollerblading down the sidewalk. "Hey, hey you! Where's the Regal Arms?"

The man stopped and thought a moment, then broke into a grin. "I don't know—connected to the Regal Shoulders?" He bent his head and gazed through the Volkswagen's window. "Cool car, dude," he said.

"Thanks," muttered Peter, but the man was already skating away.

Mattie then asked a woman who thought the Regal Arms was an East Indian restaurant that sat right next to a New Age Bookstore just down the street from an incense shop called Purple Haze. The next person he asked, a male college student with a Stanford University sweatshirt and a guitar bag slung over his shoulder, insisted that the Regal Arms was a Medieval-style restaurant, where customers ordered flagons of "mead" and the waitresses were called wenches.

Before Mattie could stop anyone else, Byte's hand came over the seat and tapped on his shoulder. "Better idea," she said. "Let's ask an older person, someone who might have been around here a while and remembers. Someone like—*him*."

Peter's eyes followed Byte's finger as it pointed. A man was sitting at the bus stop. He looked to be about fifty, and he was flipping through the pages of a newspaper. Occasionally he glanced up at the tourists who passed by, marked by their camcorders and shopping bags, and grumbled to himself behind their backs.

"Good idea," said Peter. "Wait here a sec. I'll talk to him."

He left the car and threaded his way through the traffic stopped at the red light. The man glanced up at his

196 approach, and when it was apparent that Peter was walking in his direction, he folded his newspaper and centered his gaze on the boy.

"Hello," said Peter.

"'Lo," said the man.

"Um," said Peter, "my friends and I are looking for a hotel called the Regal Arms. Do you know where it is?"

The man chuckled. "Regal Arms? Boy, did you sure miss your check-in time. There hasn't been a Regal Arms around here since before you were born."

Bingo, thought Peter.

"Yup," said the man. "They had some trouble back in the seventies—what with the oil crisis and everything, people not traveling as much, inflation being so bad. Some company bought the hotel out. It's changed names three or four times since."

"Great," said Peter. "You mean the hotel building itself is still in this neighborhood? It just has a different name?"

"Righto," said the man. He pointed down the street. "Second light, turn left. The Lamplighter Inn. That's the old Regal Arms."

Peter thanked the man and ran back to his car. He opened the driver's side door and smiled at his friends. "Come on," he said. "We're going to the Lamplighter Inn."

Derek Bellows listened as the doors to the Volkswagen slammed shut. *So*, he thought, *they're moving*. He had followed them into the hotel district, and he had listened as they discussed their problems locating the Regal Arms. Mostly, he had waited.

Now it was time for him to move as well.

He reached over to the glove compartment and twisted the knob. The glove compartment opened, and Derek's fingers grasped the heavy object that lay inside.

The object was his father's .44 caliber revolver, modeled after the ancient, western-style Smith and Wessons carried by men of the Old West. Franklin Bellows fancied himself a bit of a cowboy. When Derek was barely eleven, his father had taken him to a shooting range and, in one of his lame attempts to "make a true Bellows" out of Derek, had insisted he fire this very weapon. The recoil had been so strong the gun had arced backward and struck Derek a light blow to the forehead.

Derek took the gun now, tucked it in his belt, then adjusted his sport coat to hide the weapon. In a few moments he would be handling it like a seasoned pro. What a shame dear old Dad wasn't here to watch.

"I've never even *heard* of Growler Morton."

The clerk behind the counter of the Lamplighter Inn looked to be no more than twenty-five years old. He wore a white shirt and tie and a rumpled suit draped blanketlike over his thin frame. He stared down his thin nose at the work before him, ignoring the Misfits. Peter didn't take the rudeness personally. He and his friends looked on, silent, as the man tried to unsnag a roll of paper from a fax machine and sliced his finger on the edge of the paper cutter. He pressed a tissue against his fingertip, then looked up again at the Misfits.

"Are you still here?" he asked.

"Listen," said Peter, "we just want to look inside a room. That's *all*. In 1957 a guy was murdered at this hotel, and we're just trying—"

"Murdered?" the clerk hissed. "Listen, I don't know what you kids are up to, but I don't have time for this, okay? You want a room, rent one. You want to study history, there's a library down the block." An elderly man was mopping the floor in a corner of the lobby, and the young clerk looked over and shouted at him. "Hey— *hey!*" He pointed to a large, dull spot on the tile, yards from where the custodian was working. "Make sure you get that spot there!"

The clerk returned to his struggle with the fax machine, swearing lightly under his breath as his efforts put a jagged tear in the paper.

Mattie's attention had drifted. Instead of listening while Peter argued with the jerk behind the desk, the youngest Misfit found himself gazing at the elderly custodian. The man was wearing dark green coveralls, and he was hunched over an aluminum pail set on thick rubber wheels.

Before mopping another section of tile, the custodian gazed up at a fluorescent ceiling light that flickered off and on. He frowned, and with his eyes locked on the light fixture, reached into a pocket in the bib of his coveralls for a stick of chewing gum. Mattie watched as the man slowly unwrapped the gum, gazed at it, and crumpled the stick into his mouth. Then the old guy did something that made Mattie move a little closer: The custodian took the gum wrapper, made of metallic foil, and methodically folded it into a tiny square. He then grabbed the small stepladder hanging from his cart and set it beneath the light fixture. He climbed up the ladder, reached his hand into the fixture, and placed the folded gum wrapper into the connection.

The light stopped flickering. It even seemed to be burning a bit more brightly.

Mattie nodded a greeting to the man. Smiling, he walked over and stood patiently as the man stepped from the ladder and began sweeping the mop across another section of floor.

"Hi," he said.

The man looked at him, then dropped his gaze back to the floor. "Hi."

"I hope I'm not bothering you," said Mattie. "I'm just waiting around for my friends to solve a little problem they're having with the desk clerk."

The man grunted—or was it a laugh?—and squeezed more dirty water from the mop.

Mattie saw the thick ring of keys dangling from the man's belt. He looked at the man's face again, at the wrinkles gathered around the man's eyes, and suddenly had the suspicion that this custodian was an institution at the hotel, that he had worked here since practically the beginning of time. Mattie thought about that a moment, then let his voice drop to a whisper. "Gee," he said, glancing at the desk clerk, "I bet it must be hard taking orders from someone so young. I mean, I bet you know twice as much as he does," he said casually, "about the hotel and what's going on in it."

"Hmph," said the man. He did not look up from his mopping, but he slowed a bit.

"He comes across as a little arrogant, I guess," said Mattie. "Taking orders from him wouldn't be so bad, I figure, if he were just a little *nicer* about it. I don't know, maybe say 'please' or 'thank you' now and then, right?"

"Being polite never hurt anyone," agreed the man.

"*Exactly*," said Mattie. "Like right now. All my friends and I want to do is look around one of the rooms, and that clerk is being really rude to us. He doesn't have to act that way. We're not going to hurt anything."

The man stood, his back hunched slightly, the mop wavering as he leaned against it. He gazed at the desk clerk, and his lips pulled up in a very faint smile. "Well," he said, "I guess it would really get his goat, then, if someone was to let you and your friends into that room, wouldn't it?"

Mattie grinned and motioned for the others, who rushed over and crowded around the man.

"So, what are you all looking for?" asked the custodian, leaning again on his mop handle.

Peter smiled, instantly liking the old guy. "The answer to a forty-year-old mystery."

"Do you like jazz?" asked Jake. The question hung in the air, faintly teasing.

The custodian did not answer right away. Peter glanced to where the desk clerk was working. The clerk was darting from one unfinished task to another. If they were going to search the room, now was a good time.

The custodian smiled. "Well," he said, "now that you got me curious, then yeah, I might have a minute or two."

The Misfits followed him to room one twenty-three. The custodian knocked on the door to make sure the room was unoccupied, then pulled out a master key and fit it into the lock. He nudged the door with his finger, and it silently swung open.

The room, Peter thought, seemed typical of those found at comfortable, mid-range hotels. He saw two double beds, an inexpensive chest of drawers, a mirror, and a small writing desk where traveling businessmen could work at their laptops. On the wall between the beds was a framed poster reprint of a seascape painting.

Jake gazed at one object after another. "So this is it," he said. "This is where Growler Morton lived his last days."

Byte frowned. "But this isn't the way the room would have looked in 1957," she said. "I mean—not just the furnishings, but the carpet, the paint, everything's too modern and new."

"That's right," replied the custodian. "The carpets are replaced every few years. The rooms are painted every couple of years. Even the bathroom fixtures, the shower enclosure and such, have probably been replaced who knows how many times since the fifties. Stuff just doesn't last that long, and if it does, it doesn't look so good."

Byte turned toward Peter. "Well, if that's the case, how can we expect to find anything? This room's been torn apart and redone at least half a dozen times. If Growler Morton had left something here, it surely would have been found by now."

Peter reluctantly agreed with that assessment. However, he was not quite ready to give up hope. Growler's clues had clearly led them here.

"If something had been found earlier," he said, "then it seems likely that Growler's disappearance would have been solved at that time—unless one of the guys who had it in for Growler got to the clue first. But since that would end our search, we might as well proceed under the assumption that whatever Growler left here has not been found."

"Not in forty years?" asked Byte.

"It's a possibility," Peter replied. He frowned, thinking. "We've come this far, and we have nothing to lose by trying. Let's concentrate on the last clue. There's got to be something in the song lyrics, something we haven't figured out yet."

Jake reached into his pocket for the folded sheet of notepaper on which he had written the lyrics to Growler's waltz.

"What are some of the key phrases?" Peter asked.

Jake stared down at the sheet. "Well, they're 'beneath the moon'—"

"Hey," said Mattie, "the moon—could that maybe refer to a light fixture?" He pointed toward the ceiling, where a large lamp hung from a brass chain.

Byte thought for a moment, then shook her head. "I don't think so," she said. "Growler would want Mrs. Morton to get the message, and understanding from that one mention that he meant the lamp—I don't know, that would be a real leap. He couldn't be sure she'd understand it."

Peter watched Jake walk along the room's perimeter, his eyes focused as if he were concentrating on a musical composition. Jake's hand touched the wall here and there, finally stopping at a small vent near the ceiling. Jake held his fingers up to the vent, waggling them in the cold air that blew in through the central air-conditioning system.

He laughed and turned to the others. "Hey," he said. "I have a really freaky idea. The only lyric that repeats in every verse is 'I'll waltz with Helen where the cool breeze blows.' Maybe Growler hid the bonds *inside the air-conditioning*."

Mattie reached into his jacket pocket and pulled out his multi-tool. He threw a questioning glance at the custodian, and the custodian nodded his permission. Mattie then selected a screwdriver bit and, getting a helpful boost from Jake, removed the screws from the vent. Beneath the grate was a cardboard filter, which he removed as well. "I can just squeeze inside," he said, and, grinning, he looked back down at the others. "Hey, just like in the movies."

Byte tugged at Peter's sleeve. "Please tell me that he's not going to fall through that vent and break his neck," she whispered.

Peter shrugged.

Jake held Mattie's legs as the smaller boy slid into the vent. He wriggled through headfirst, and he pushed inside until all Peter saw were his knees and lower legs. A metallic pop came from within the wall as Mattie's weight shifted along the aluminum vent. This movement lasted several seconds and was followed by a bark. The barking sound was Mattie coughing. "Okay," he called, "pull me out." His voice in the wall sounded distant and muffled. Jake gripped him by the ankles and yanked him out in one long pull.

Mattie coughed some more. He looked up at the others, his jacket and pants coated with fine dust. "I'm sorry, guys," he said. "Really. But there's nothing in there."

Peter shook his head. "That's impossible." He could admit to being wrong at times, but he couldn't imagine being *this* wrong. *Regal Arms, room 123, where the cool breeze blows....* He tried backtracking over all their conclusions, looking for a mistake, for other possibilities, but none came to him.

"Now wait," said a voice. The custodian walked to the center of the room, and he nodded to himself. "Yes," he said. "I remember now. This is a central heat-and-air system; one big pump sends air to every room in the hotel. Back then, though, we didn't have central. Every room had its own separate wall unit."

"Where would the wall unit have been?" asked Peter.

The custodian looked around the room, his forehead crinkling into deep furrows. After several moments, he threw his arms up in a great, heaving shrug.

Mattie got down on his knees and began moving around the room, thumping the wall here and there with his fingers.

"What are you doing?" asked Byte.

"Looking for a hollow spot," he replied. "Some large spot where I don't hear a support beam." He crawled along the floor, leaving a trail of chalk-colored dust in the carpet as he listened for a deep, hollow place where the old air-conditioner would have rested. He covered most of the room, except one large portion of wall covered by a dresser and vanity mirror.

"I got it," said Jake. He gripped one side of the dresser, lifted it, and angled it away from the wall. Then he gripped the other side and pulled it away as well.

Peter, Jake, and Byte got on their knees and joined Mattie, watching him as he ran his fingers over the painted drywall. He discovered a barely discernible line, a seam, that ran up from the floor, crossed the wall, then ran back down. It formed a square about three feet on each side.

"That's it," said the custodian. "When they took out the old units, they just cut a section of drywall big enough to match the hole, set it in, then covered the seam with a special tape. Once they repainted, you could hardly tell the hole was there."

206 Peter looked at the man, and the custodian seemed to read his mind. "Well, go on," he said, gesturing toward the wall. "Do what you got to do. I can always fix it."

"Mattie?"

"Right." Mattie selected a bladed screwdriver with a sharp edge. He knelt down next to Peter and dug the edge of the blade into the wall. He ran the blade along the seam as though slitting an envelope with a letter opener. Peter dug his fingers into the gap and tugged. In seconds, a three-foot square section of drywall peeled off with a light tear. What remained was an opening of black tar paper and two-by-four studs.

Mattie reached inside the opening. He felt around, but the motion of his arm stopped after only a second or two. Peter looked at him, and the younger boy smiled. Jake pumped his fist in the air, and Byte took a step forward, unable to contain herself.

"Well?" she demanded.

Mattie grinned. "I've got something."

"Good," said a voice from behind them. "Now you can give it to me."

Peter turned around, and there, leaning in the doorway, was Derek Bellows. The record company executive looked at the group and smiled. "Heyyy," he said.

He didn't have to form his fingers into the shape of a gun, Peter noted. He was holding a real one this time.

Jake took a half step sideways toward Bellows. Bellows caught the move and swiveled the gun in Jake's direction.

"Don't even think about it," Bellows said. Then he turned to Peter. "Well, go on," he said. "I've been thinking about those bonds for a long time now. I'm really happy you've found them for me."

Peter saw Bellows's throat muscles convulse. The man was nervous, which would make him all the more unpredictable and dangerous.

Mattie slowly withdrew his arm from the wall. "It's not the bonds." When his hand came free, it held what appeared to be a small, leather-bound book. He handed it to Peter. Peter looked at Bellows, and when Bellows nodded at him, Peter flipped through the book's pages.

"It's a journal or something," Peter announced. "There's writing all through it...it appears to be Growler's handwriting."

He turned to the last few pages and began to read silently to himself. From the first paragraph, he felt a tingling in his chest. Peter could almost hear the man's voice speaking to him from the page.

August 12, 1957
Dear Helen,
All I can hope for is that I can hide this journal here until you find it—and that you'll understand why I had to leave. You're in my thoughts every moment of every day. Please believe that. I can't bear to think of what must be going through your mind right now.

Part of me wishes I had left this book at home for you. But the person who stole the bonds will do anything—kill me, kill you—to avoid being caught. For now, you're safer not knowing the whole truth. And since I have the book with me, I can explain everything that's happening.

Take care of my things, and you'll find this. Someday you'll find this…and you'll know….

Peter lost himself in the book, flipping through its final pages until his eyes fell on a name. He stared at the name for several moments, nodding to himself. *Of course,* he thought, *it makes perfect sense.* Growler *had* known the truth. Peter's silence grew long and he began to sense impatience from across the room. When he looked up, Bellows leveled the gun in his direction.

"All right, that's enough," Bellows said. "Give it to me."

Peter nodded. "Fine," he said quietly. "I think you probably need to read this more than I do." He tossed the book gently into the air and watched as it landed in Bellows's free hand. The record company executive looked closely at each of the Misfits, and especially at Peter.

"Don't try anything," he warned.

Bellows opened the book and began to read. Peter watched, fascinated. The man's face turned red, then a bloodless white. Seeing the changes in his appearance was like watching a photograph as Byte morphed it on her computer. .

He began shaking his head back and forth, then he sank to the floor and let the gun drop from his fingers. His head rested against his knees and he gazed at the wall, his eyes vacant.

Peter walked over and carefully picked up the gun. He handed it to Jake, then knelt down next to Bellows and waited until the man's eyes became clear again. He brushed his hair back from his forehead because he wanted Derek Bellows to see his own eyes, his own determination.

"Now that we know the truth," Peter said, "we need to set straight forty years of lies. Will you help us?"

Bellows remained silent for a few moments while the Misfits waited. And then, slowly closing the book, he began to nod.

eleven

Saturday

the following afternoon, when the Misfits arrived at RSA Records, Derek Bellows was waiting for them in the lobby. Peter noted his blank facial expression and the odd wildness in his eyes.

"Are you ready for this?" asked Peter.

Bellows nodded. "As ready as I can be."

They turned toward the elevator, but standing in their path was the elderly woman Peter remembered from the first time he and Mattie had visited RSA—Agnes was her name. She stood before them in a lace-collared dress and cardigan sweater, her shoulders hunched, her eyes spearing Derek as she approached. But then she stopped. Her eyes flitted back and forth across Derek and the Misfits. She raised her hand, pointing a gnarled finger at the record executive.

"Your guests *did* sign in with the receptionist, Mr. Bellows?" Her voice dripped with disdain.

Derek paused. He looked at the old woman, and Peter

thought he saw the corners of Derek's mouth tug upward ever so slightly. "You know what, Agnes?" he said, his voice gentle, and, Peter thought, almost kind. "Ever since I started working here, you've treated me like I was one step below plankton on the food chain. You've looked down your nose at me and generally showed me the respect you would show someone with a tattoo, several body piercings, and a criminal record."

The woman's rhinestone-studded eyeglasses dangled around her neck by a gold chain. She reached for them now and drew them onto her face, studying Derek with a puzzled expression.

"—It's okay," Derek went on. "I don't blame you. I hadn't done much to earn anyone's respect." The faint tugging at his mouth grew more apparent. Derek Bellows was smiling. "But don't worry. Starting this afternoon, the whole world changes." He gave Agnes's cheek two light pats with his hand and strode past her to the elevator.

Derek and the Misfits rode the elevator silently to the twelfth floor. When the door finally swished open, the group faced a long, marble-floored hallway. Peter noted the lines of gold lacing through the marble's surface. The five of them walked down it, their footsteps drumming like a basketball in an empty gym.

Besides the receptionist, Agnes, and Franklin Bellows, the RSA building would be empty this morning. Derek had assured the Misfits that the elder Bellows often finished his week's work on Saturday morning, and he demanded that a small clerical staff join him.

At the end of the hallway they came to a heavy, unmarked door. Derek Bellows paused, took a deep breath, and flung the door open.

Franklin Bellows was behind his desk. He looked up as the group entered, a sheaf of papers rustling in his fingers. Peter watched him measure the scene.

"Well, Derek," he finally said, "this is quite unannounced."

Derek strode to the desk. "Dad," he said, "these people have a few things to discuss with you. I'd like to sit in."

"And the subject of this discussion—?"

"Growler Morton," said Peter.

Bellows set the papers down on the desktop, his hand quivering slightly. Though the trembling passed quickly, Peter caught it. He was sure the other Misfits had too.

"Let's start with the missing bonds," Peter said. "Growler Morton didn't steal them. You did."

Bellows's face went pale.

"As you remember," Peter went on, "we've been investigating Mr. Morton's disappearance. We hadn't learned very much—which you were probably counting on— but yesterday evening we found something that filled in most of the gaps. You see, Mr. Bellows, Growler Morton left a diary."

Franklin Bellows stared across the desk at Peter. His shoulders tensed, then relaxed as he reached for the pen in his gold desk set. He calmly scribbled his signature across the bottom of one of sheets he had been perusing.

"Growler Morton was having money problems," Peter persisted. "Your son said so, Mrs. Morton said so, and the diary confirmed it. He enjoyed gambling, and he got himself heavily in debt to the organized crime members who owned the casinos."

"They were threatening to hurt him," added Jake. "Him *and* his wife."

"Right," said Peter. "Growler got scared and decided to hide out, but before he left he wanted to leave a message for his wife. A message only she would understand. He left it in three parts—one note in a clarinet, one in the sleeve of a 45-rpm record, and the third was written into Growler's last musical composition. What's interesting is that, when Growler disappeared, those three items showed up in a newspaper photograph. It was public knowledge that he had made a point of leaving them behind."

Bellows leaned back in his chair.

When a half-smile crossed the record executive's face, Peter felt the muscles in his own jaw tense. The man's arrogance almost cracked the cool, logical image that Peter loved to project. Bellows's contemptuous calm made Peter want to reach across the desk and shake the man by the lapels of his thousand-dollar suit.

"Well, it seems to me you're building quite a case against Growler," the executive said. "Not against me."

Peter did not return the smile. "There's more. In an interview after Growler's disappearance, you said, 'He was more than a musician we had under contract here, he was my friend.' That wasn't exactly true, was it? The truth was, Growler was planning to leave RSA for another record label. A few days before he disappeared, you and he argued, and Growler hit you. Mrs. Morton told us that's how you got the scar on your cheek—from the stone in Growler's ring."

Bellows shrugged.

"But there was something important she didn't know, wasn't there? She didn't know that the punch *knocked the stone out of the ring.* You hated Growler for leaving the label, and you saw a chance to grab three million for yourself while blaming him, so you planted the stone near the safe and stole the bonds yourself. It was a perfect set-up. *You* knew the trouble he was in with the mob. *You* knew he wouldn't survive it. He'd take the heat for the theft, you'd get three million in bonds, and RSA wouldn't even be out the money because the company insurance policy would cover the theft."

Peter felt his face flush with anger. As he was speaking, his every word nailing Bellows like a needle through the chest of an insect specimen, the record executive *chuckled.* Peter began to speak faster and louder.

"His diary explained that he was hiding out because of his debts. When the stories appeared about the bonds being stolen, and about the stone being found by the safe, Growler knew you'd set him up. By then, the mobsters were getting close. Growler couldn't clear his name without being found by the mob, so he waited. But I guess he waited too long. Just before the mobsters found him, he hid his diary behind the air-conditioner in the hotel room where he and his wife had honeymooned. His clues had told her she could find it there."

Bellows sat in his chair, silent. The look of smug superiority drained from his face.

"Is all this true, Dad?" asked Derek. When his father didn't answer, he exploded. "*Say something!*"

"Derek," said Bellows, his voice low and hoarse, "this is of no concern to you. I want you to leave."

"I'm not leaving," said Derek. "Not until I hear everything."

"You know what I'm curious about?" asked Peter. "I'm curious about what happened to Growler's body after he was thrown off the hotel roof. You know—the way his face was battered? The fingertips cut off and all? Did you have something to do with that?"

Bellows froze, then spat out his response. "Are you suggesting I was involved in a murder?"

Peter shook his head. "I'm just wondering—did you have connections with some of those mob people, Mr. Bellows? You see, I'm no expert, but my guess is that mob types would not kill a man who owed them money. They might rough him up, but they'd want him alive until they got their money back, right? So I was just wondering. Maybe you knew someone who knew someone. You could make a phone call. It would be so easy to rationalize—Growler was already in trouble; that was a given. So maybe those boys could do you a little favor—in exchange for paying off Growler's gambling debts. Kill Growler Morton. Mess up the body so it can't be identified. Keep Growler, the jazz legend, alive a little longer, while any trail leading to you grew cold."

Bellows remained silent.

"The saddest part of this whole story," Byte said, "is that Helen Morton never discovered those clues. She never found the diary. He did everything he could to protect her, but she never understood."

"Right," said Jake. "It took forty years for everything to come out in the open. What started the whole thing—the thefts and violence, I mean—was Mrs. Morton's decision to have an auction. As long as the three clues were in her possession—and as long as she remained, well, clueless about them—*you* had no problem. But her auction brought back all those old news stories about Growler. He was all over the media—again. People were thinking about Growler's disappearance, asking new questions, and you started to worry. Did Growler leave any evidence or clues that might point to you?"

"And you remembered the old photo, didn't you, Mr. Bellows?" said Byte. "You didn't know for sure that Growler had tried to warn Helen about what was going on, but you must have suspected. When you heard about the auction, you worried that the items in the photo would be auctioned off and some sort of clue discovered. So you made up your mind to get them. If they were worthless, then you were just out some money. But if they contained something incriminating, then you would be the only one to know."

"So you hired Karl Logan to steal them," added Jake, "just to save your own skin."

At the mention of the thief's name, Franklin Bellows maintained his calm, but Peter noted the beads of perspiration forming along the man's forehead and neck.

"Exactly," said Peter. "But Logan's plans didn't work out. He didn't know that someone else had made the connection between the three items. *We* were looking for clues as well. Logan discovered that when he ran into Jake at Mrs. Morton's home, the night he shot Scott Morton."

Bellows sat back in his chair. Peter knew he had unnerved the man, but he also knew that Bellows had been thinking as well as listening. The executive sipped from a mug of coffee, uncaring, the anger and fear completely gone from his face.

A moment later he revealed the source of his peace of mind. "Young man," Bellows said, "you have cobbled together quite a bit of circumstantial evidence, but you cannot *prove* anything. Would you like to know how I know that?" He reached for his mug and took another sip of coffee, his hand steady as he spoke. "I assume you've taken your 'evidence,' the journal you mentioned finding, to the police," he went on. "The reason the police are not here with you now is because they told you about the statute of limitations."

Peter was quiet. Bellows had them, almost as though he had read Peter's mind. Yes, the Misfits had indeed brought Growler Morton's journal to Lieutenant Decker. Decker had explained to them, in very clear terms, the statute of limitations. In law enforcement, the police had a "deadline" for solving a crime—three years for a misdemeanor, seven years for a felony. If they went past that deadline, they could no longer bring the case to court. The case of the missing bonds was forty years old; and now, though it was solved, it would have to remain buried. The Misfits could certainly embarrass Franklin Bellows. They could devastate his reputation. But unless they could prove he murdered Growler Morton—murder had no limitation, Decker had said—they would never put him behind bars.

"Well…you've committed crimes more recently," Peter offered. He tried to keep the uncertainty out of his voice. "You conspired with Karl Logan to commit robberies."

"Absolutely untrue," said Bellows. "Do you have testimony from this Karl Logan? No? I'm afraid, young man, that you have nothing against me at all, and I've finally reached the end of my patience. You and your friends will leave now, or I'll have security escort you out."

Peter looked at Bellows, then at his friends. He jerked his head in the direction of the door, and the Misfits quietly gathered their belongings and left.

On the way to the elevator, Peter felt his stomach knot. "You know what?" he muttered, loud enough for all the Misfits to hear. "That guy makes me want to throw up." He strode through the marble hallway, his fist pounding absently against the wall, the sound echoing. "What kind of world allows someone like that, so arrogant in his big office and leather chair, to step right over everything that's right…and fair…and just?" Peter choked on the words, furious. In the movies, bad guys always paid in the end for their crimes. Peter knew the real world didn't always work that way, but the fact had never slapped him in the face before.

As he strode down the hall, Byte hurried to catch up with him. She eyed him for a moment, then gazed ahead, keeping pace with him as he walked. For a long time she said nothing. Peter glanced at her—sensing she was searching for words—then turned his attention to the elevator doors at the end of the long hallway. All he wanted now was to leave the building, to get as far away as he could from the evil smell of this place.

Byte nudged him with her hip. "Hey," she whispered, "are you going to be all right?"

Peter stared down at the floor, wishing he could spy a pebble or an empty soft drink can, something he could kick down the length of the hallway. But the marble floor with the gold lacing was spotless.

Jake and Mattie, walking a few steps ahead, suddenly broke into a run and raced each other to the elevator. Jake won easily, slamming his palm down on the call button.

"You know," Byte went on, "if it makes any difference…I'm really proud of the way you figured everything out, and the way you stood up to that creep in there."

Peter said nothing.

Byte nudged him again. "It *does* make a difference, doesn't it?" she insisted. "I mean, what *I* think? You did a great job."

Peter thought again about Franklin Bellows—the smug way his smile curled up on only one side of his mouth, like someone who knew a dirty secret about you. He thought about the fact that a man who might very well have been involved in a murder—though Peter had no proof—would likely go unpunished.

These thoughts must have made Peter's expression even more unhappy, because Byte slung one arm around his neck and pulled him to her, half-choking him. "Okay," she said, "it works likes this. I quit squeezing your neck when you're ready to smile and admit that you did good work. Understand?"

"Urgh?" said Peter.

"I said, *Do…you…understand?*" repeated Byte, emphasizing each word.

"Ah uggathan! Ah uggathan!"

Byte kept the arm tight as she continued. "Good," she said. "Because I would hate to think that the smartest guy I've ever known was feeling down on himself. It wouldn't be right."

Peter offered no more objections, and she released him. He stood up straight, rubbing his sore neck. "Okay," he said, grinning, "that's it. You're not watching WWF over at Jake's anymore."

Jake and Mattie were still several yards away, eyeing Peter and Byte and rolling their eyes. The elevator door swished as it opened behind them.

Moments later, as the Misfits were exiting the lobby, Derek Bellows pulled Peter aside. He tried to look Peter in the eyes, but his gaze kept dropping. "Um, listen," he said, "I'm embarrassed to explain. But when you get out to your car, you might want to take a look underneath the dash."

At the end of the day, Franklin Bellows rubbed his eyes. When he took the hand away, it was shaking. Too much caffeine. After those teenagers had left, Bellows had swallowed cup after cup of his expensive coffee.

Though he had already worked out early this morning, he stopped by his fitness club again on the way home. He ran five miles on a treadmill, punching the speed up faster and faster until he felt dizzy and nauseous. The steam room afterwards felt oppressive. His cold dip chilled him, penetrating his bones and making his body tremble.

He went to his favorite restaurant and ordered a salad and a grilled chicken breast brushed with lemon sauce. He picked at the food, paid, then left.

Once home, Bellows finally admitted to himself that the teenagers had unsettled him. He was astonished that they had discovered so much, had figured out so much of what he had done and how he had done it. But no matter. He had been right. The police could not prosecute him for a crime he committed forty years ago. Only his name, his precious name, might suffer.

He lay back on his couch, leaving the lights off because they hurt his eyes.

Something moved in the shadows. At first Bellows thought it was the draperies catching a breeze from the open window. But when the shadow moved again, he saw clearly that it was the figure of a man. Bellows bolted upright just as the man circled the couch, his face catching the pale light from outside.

"Hello, Mr. Bellows," said Karl Logan.

"I believe in treating my clients fairly," Logan said, flicking on a lamp with his gloved hand. "I expect fair treatment in return." He sat casually on the arm of Bellows's Italian leather sofa, like a friend who had come by to talk shop and share a drink.

"What do you want?" Bellows croaked.

"A little chat," replied the thief. "Just so we understand each other."

Logan walked over to an alcove and stared at a painting on the wall. He ran his finger along the top of the frame, examining it for dust. He gazed at his finger, wrinkled his nose, then wiped the finger across his pant leg.

"I broke into your office last night," Logan said. "I bypassed the security on your computer system and hacked into your bank account. You'll be pleased to know that I've now been paid in full for my services. There was a lot more money there, but I took only what you owed me."

Bellows swallowed. "I see."

"And there's something else."

Logan spoke with such calm that Bellows's whole body trembled. He sat on his couch with his knees together, his hands clasped between them like a child in fear of punishment.

"I've made contact with the authorities about the bonds you stole."

Bellows felt his breathing suddenly relax. Was Logan that stupid?

"The police can do nothing," Bellows said. "The statute of limitations...."

Logan laughed. "Do you remember Al Capone? In the 1920s he ran bootleg liquor, illegal speakeasies, gambling and prostitution parlors; he even had people murdered. The law couldn't convict him of any of those crimes, so you know what they did? They brought in an accountant. Capone hadn't paid taxes on any of the illegal money he had made. Get it? He got away with murder, but he went to jail for tax evasion."

Bellows felt a tingling at the base of his spine. It spread upward and ran along his arms and fingers.

"—I used your computer to e-mail the IRS. Check with your tax lawyers, Mr. Bellows; the law offers no statute of limitations on filing a fraudulent income tax form. So unless you paid taxes on the bonds you stole in '57, you're going to owe the IRS those taxes, plus forty years' worth of interest and penalties. I figure everything you own will just about cover the bill." Logan stood then and made his way to the window. "Get a good night's sleep, Mr. Bellows," he said. "You've got a rocky time ahead of you."

Bugle Point International Airport, six hours later

Lieutenant Decker reached into his coat pocket as he studied the airport crowd. He found the tin of aspirin in his coat pocket and popped two of them into his mouth.

The search for Karl Logan had begun within hours of his appearance at the Armstrong home. Decker had now stationed himself at one of the airport's security checkpoints. Sam had taken the other. Here, every passenger heading for a plane walked through a metal detector, and every piece of carry-on luggage passed through an X-ray machine. This process slowed the traffic enough that Decker was able to get a good look at everyone who stood in line.

He glanced down at the paper he was holding. It was a composite sheet of some of the disguises used by Karl Logan. Once the Armstrong kid had given him Logan's name and description, Decker was able to run a check on the guy. In addition to a lengthy, interesting background—which included *zero* arrests—the sheet bore twelve small photographs in all, each reproduced in enough detail that Decker felt he was sure to recognize Logan in whatever identity the guy assumed. Decker had given a copy of the sheet to every airport security officer, and he had left one at every ticket counter. Local bus depots, Amtrak stations, even car rental places received copies as well. Roadblocks covered key thoroughfares. The operation was a slam-dunk.

Someone new had joined the line. Standing behind an elderly woman was a tall man with long, red hair and a full beard. The man wore a plaid flannel shirt, and he was thin everywhere in his body except for the heavy pouch of a beer-belly that dripped over his silver belt buckle. Decker squinted. It seemed a pretty thin disguise by Karl Logan's usual standards.

While Decker eyed the newcomer, the elderly woman in front reached for her carry-on bag. Its latch came undone and the bag opened, spilling a toothbrush, a container of rose-scented bath crystals, and several ladies' underthings onto the airport carpet. Decker took advantage of the distraction. He helped the lady gather her belongings, while at the same time getting a closer look at the red-haired man.

"Oh, thank you, thank you," said the woman. She reached into her pocketbook and tried to hand Decker a dollar bill for his trouble.

"It's my pleasure," said Decker. "Keep your money."

He guided her toward her gate, glancing over his shoulder the entire time. The red-haired man was just now passing through the metal detector. The alarm sounded, and a security officer pulled the man aside and ran a wand across him, checking him for weapons. After a brief conversation about the man's wallet, the security officer let the man go.

Decker excused himself from the woman, then stepped back and leaned against the wall, waiting casually for the man to reach him. When the man did,

Decker flashed his badge. "Bugle Point P.D. May I see your identification, please?"

"Aw, man, what is this? Do I look like a terrorist or something?" The man reached into his pocket and pulled out a black leather wallet with chrome snaps and a silver chain. The wallet bore a Harley-Davidson logo. "First they give me a hard time because my chain messes with their metal detector, and now this. We're turning into a Fascist country, man, I'm telling you."

He pulled out his driver's license and handed it to Decker. It looked good. According to the file, Logan was supposed to be a master at creating phony documents, but Decker considered himself equally masterful at spotting them. If this was a fake, it was better than any fake Decker had ever seen.

"Now take it easy," Decker said. There was one other test he had to try before he would be satisfied the man was not Logan. He reached for a handful of the man's hair, and gently, so he didn't pull it, raised the hair so he could see where it met the scalp. If the man were wearing a wig, or hair extensions, Decker would know.

"Man, what are you doing—?"

The hair grew right out of the man's natural scalp. Decker handed back the driver's license. "You can go," he said. "Sorry for the inconvenience."

Decker took a deep breath and leaned against the wall again. Logan would try to get through here. Decker was certain. Catching him was only a matter of being patient—and watchful.

Frowning, he glanced at the elderly woman stepping onto the gangway. He studied her as she shuffled toward the waiting plane.

Nah, Decker thought. *It couldn't be....*

Karl Logan guided his new boat away from the dock and into the waters of the Bugle Point Marina. The pilot's cabin stood high and well forward in the craft, and Logan loved how it gave him a clear view of the bow and the choppy sea ahead of him.

A jet rose from the distant airport, and Logan watched it climb into the sky, heading off to whatever destination awaited it. He found himself staring at it as it flew overhead.

Once he cleared the crowded bay, Logan pointed the boat into open waters. The salt spray licked at his hair and lightly stung his cheeks. He drew in a deep breath, savoring it. The entire Pacific Ocean lay before him—without walls, without bars, without the gaze of the police.

Logan's cell phone chirped. He picked it up, gazed at it a moment, and tossed it over the side.

epilogue

Sunday

Jake held Growler Morton's weathered journal in his hand. He also held the sheet music to "Waltz with Helen." It was time to return them both. He looked at the other Misfits, took a deep breath, and knocked on Helen Morton's front door. This was not going to be an easy job.

A light, rhythmic creaking came from the other side of the door, growing steadily louder. Jake recognized it. It was Scott Morton moving through the hallway on his crutches. The door opened a moment later, and Scott greeted them.

"Come on in," he said. "Mom's been waiting."

He led the Misfits to the den. Mrs. Morton was stacking the last of the boxes for the movers. Jake suspected that she was staying busy for the sake of staying busy, keeping her hands and mind occupied.

"Hello," she said. "Thank you all for coming." Peter, Byte, and Mattie shook her hand, but when Jake approached, she clasped his hand in both of hers and held it for a few moments.

They all sat—Helen, Scott, and the Misfits—and Jake began the story of how Franklin Bellows had betrayed Growler Morton. He explained the clues Growler had left and how the Misfits had deciphered them. Last, he told her of Growler's death, glossing over the violent details. He saw no sense in the woman suffering any more than she already had.

"The clues led us to this," Jake said. He handed the journal to Mrs. Morton. "It explains everything." He paused, a little embarrassed. "And, well, it talks a lot about you. We only read the last few pages. Just enough to, you know, learn what happened at the end."

Helen Morton wrapped her arms around the book and clutched it to her chest, as if she were hugging Growler himself. "I remember this book," she said. "Growler used to write in it all the time. He would never let me read it."

"Well," said Jake softly, "I'm sure he wouldn't mind if you read it now."

Mrs. Morton ran her fingers over the binding. She lifted the cover, then let it fall back into place, unable to turn to the first page. Her hands squeezed the book.

"You know," said Byte. "There's something really ironic about all this. Everyone was trying to solve those clues, and we were all so certain we were going to find the missing bonds. But the bonds were long gone. And the clues weren't about money at all. They were about you finding your way back to Growler. I guess you got the answer to your question, Mrs. Morton. Your husband really did love you."

Helen Morton squeezed her eyes shut, then opened them again to gaze at the journal. After a moment, she turned to the first page and began to read. Jake, watching her, grew more and more uncomfortable in the long silence. It seemed wrong to be watching, like eavesdropping during an intimate conversation. It seemed a good time, Jake thought, for the Misfits to excuse themselves. He set the sheet music down on the coffee table, shot a quick glance at his friends, and they all rose to leave.

Helen Morton sat on the couch next to her son, her fingers rubbing absently over the journal's yellowed pages.

"Wait," she said. They turned. "Young man," she said, her gaze fixed solidly on Jake, "you play, don't you? I mean, that's what started all this. You're a horn player."

Jake nodded.

"Then I want you to have something."

She rose from the couch and strode toward the cedar chest in the center of the room. Kneeling, she reached into the chest and pulled out an old clarinet case.

She handed the case to Jake. "This was Growler's favorite. The clarinet you bought was an old one, the one he played when we first met—I suppose that's why he slipped his message into it. This is the one he performed with later, the one he used in his recordings."

Jake took the case, his hands shaking. He looked at Mrs. Morton, unable to speak, and she nodded her encouragement. Jake set the case on a coffee table, ran his fingers along the seam, and popped the latch.

The clarinet was like the one he'd bought at the auction—if that one had died and gone to heaven, reborn as something…perfect. It shimmered. The four parts of the body were glistening, polished ebony. The keys were ten-karat gold. Over time the gold had darkened, but the antiquing gave the instrument a look of age and character. Jake would never polish it.

"It's yours under two conditions," said Mrs. Morton. "First, you must promise to always keep it.…"

"Forever," whispered Jake.

"And," said Mrs. Morton, "you must play for me."

Jake swallowed hard. "*Now?*"

She nodded.

"Right this minute? I'm not sure I can." He felt light-headed. What could he play? He tried to remember the jazz pieces he was working on in band class, but they all seemed too meaningless, too inconsequential for the weight of this moment.

Then Jake's eyes fell on the table where he had laid the sheets of Growler's music. He glanced at Mrs. Morton, and the woman froze. She hesitated, then stood a little taller. Without a word, she sat down on the couch and waited.

Jake fumbled in his coat pocket for a reed. A clarinet reed was a fragile, bamboo-like bit of wood, often splitting and becoming useless. Serious woodwind players like Jake carried reeds the way a guitarist might carry around a handful of thin, plastic guitar picks. Jake took a new reed from its transparent container and placed it in his mouth to moisten it. When he was sure it was ready, he unscrewed the clarinet's ligature and inserted the reed into the instrument. Drawing in a deep breath, he looked down at the music and brought the clarinet to his lips.

Then he began to play.

Growler's simple tune was sweet, low, and so very sad. It saturated the air, and like all good music, it formed images in the minds of its listeners: a lone man in a snapbrim hat, silhouetted beneath the yellow glare of a corner lamppost…a wedding bouquet tossed in the air with pink ribbon trailing, outstretched fingers waiting to catch it …a woman in a taffeta dress, waltzing alone.

Through it all, Helen Morton listened—her eyes closed, tears streaming down her cheeks, hearing, finally, Growler Morton's last declaration of love.